The Sleeping Sword

ISBN 0-9775807-0-9

Cover design by Marcus Toyne

The
Sleeping
Sword

M. J. Toyne

Prologue

(Briton 1500 years ago)

BOOM, BOOM!

The pounding on the abbey doors echoed down the corridor. Sister Beatrice, annoyed that her duties as doorkeeper had called her away from the room Queen Guinevere was occupying, hurried towards it as quickly as she could without appearing unseemly.

BOOM, BOOM!

Assigning herself a penance for some unkind thoughts about people knocking on doors in the middle of the night, she reached up, opened a small hatch and peered out.

The flickering torch light barely illuminated the figure outside but it was enough to see it was a man dressed in the plain robes worn by the few druids that still held sway in some regions. Behind him was a matronly village woman.

The druid's hood was up concealing his face, but it could only be one person.

She un-barred the door and let them in.

"Am I too late?" the figure enquired.

"I don't know seeing as I'm here at the door and not in the room with the good lady."

"You'd better add a couple of 'Hail Mary's' to your other penance for that answer. Now show us the way."

Rattled by his seeming knowledge of her, Beatrice could do nothing but comply.

◇◇◇◇◇◇

Sweat trickled down Guinevere's face. It had been five hours now and the pain was definitely getting

1

worse. She wanted to get up and walk about. She wanted a back rub. She was sure that a nice warm bath would help.

A nun, one of several in the room, gently dabbed at the sweat with a cloth.

"There, there. You just lie quietly. It's the best thing."

Guinevere's reply turned to a groan as another contraction began.

◇◇◇◇◇◇

The groan caused Beatrice to frown and increase her pace.

The village woman glanced towards the druid. "Sounds like we're just in time," she said as they hurried to keep up.

◇◇◇◇◇◇

The nun was starting to suspect that dabbing with a cloth was, in fact, no help and that maybe reading a Psalm would be appropriate.

"Get me someone who knows what they're doing," Guinevere thought as she noticed the nun reaching for a Bible.

As if in answer the door to the chamber opened.

The druid pushed past Beatrice and strode toward the bed where he pulled back his hood releasing a mane of white hair and a long flowing beard.

"Merlin!" Guinevere gasped. "Thank God."

The nuns gasped in surprise except for Beatrice who muttered "Novices" under her breath.

The village woman looked at her. "You don't seem surprised?"

"What other druid would be out and about to visiting. Just because I'm a nun doesn't mean I don't know what goes on outside these walls."

Merlin leant over Guinevere.

"I've brought help."

She gripped his hand in thanks and then nearly

crushed it as another contraction took hold.

"Oooohhhhhh!"

This was the village woman's cue. She stepped forward, rolling up her sleeves and taking stock. She addressed the gathered nuns.

"Now which of you has any experience with childbirth?"

None of them stirred.

"Thought not." She turned to Beatrice. "And you?"

"Second eldest in a family of ten," Beatrice replied.

The woman nodded. "You'll do. The rest of you, clear out."

A glare from Merlin backed up the woman's command and they scurried out.

"You too," she said to Merlin.

He began to protest but after a moment thought better of it.

"I'll keep an eye out," he muttered as he went out the door gently massaging his bruised hand.

"And close it behind you," the midwife called after him.

The solid clunk of the door closing was her only answer.

With a satisfied nod, she beckoned to Sister Beatrice and they turned their attention to Guinevere.

"Now let's get the good lady out of that bed and get her walking around. Then give her a back rub."

Another groan escaped from Guinevere but somehow the pain wasn't quite as unbearable as it was before.

It was later that the Mother Superior, alerted by a group of frightened nuns, made her way to the queen's room.

She was met by the sight of the queen smiling as she nursed a newborn boy in her arms.

"M'lady is well?" she enquired, bowing slightly.

"Very. Thank you."

"And the child?"

The queen smiled down at the bright pink, little face. "He's perfect."

"Then I shall make the appropriate arrangements." She bowed slightly again and began to withdraw.

"Arrangements?" the queen asked. "What arrangements?"

"I'm rather curious myself," added Merlin.

The Mother Superior frowned.

"Surely you weren't expecting to keep the child?"

"I really hadn't thought about it. I just...." She hugged the baby tighter.

"The infant shall be taken to a monastery and raised by the monks until such time as he takes holy orders himself."

"What?" Guinevere exclaimed.

"It is our way. Those born here outside of a holy union, stay in the church to atone for the sin of their existence."

"But..." Guinevere began to protest.

"It is the spawn of adultery and hateful in the sight of God."

"No HE isn't," Guinevere said. "He's definitely Arthur's. He was conceived before Lancelot and I ever..." Tears took over and Guinevere gently rocked the baby back and forth as she sobbed.

"This is the king's true son," Merlin's voice was so definite that it even startled him.

"How can you be sure?" the Mother Superior demanded.

Merlin reached down and grabbed the baby's right hand revealing a birthmark shaped like the hilt of a sword on the palm.

"This is the mark of Excalibur. Only a Pendragon, a child of Arthur or their child thereafter can bear this mark. They are the ones that..."

Merlin closed his eyes and his voice took on a resonant, prophetic tone.

"When a new age dawns and evil without home arises,

one shall be born whose mark is complete. They shall be the one who shall wield Excalibur against the evil once more. They shall be the next Pendragon."

Merlin opened his eyes. "Sorry. Did I drift off?"

"Not so as you'd notice," the midwife said with a raised eyebrow.

The Mother Superior considered what she'd just heard.

"I'm not giving you much credibility but just suppose what you say is true, why is the queen here and not at Camelot proclaiming the joyous news of a legitimate heir to the king?"

"Because there would always be doubt," Merlin said. "Even if almost all accepted him, that lone voice of doubt would be enough to undermine and prevent him from doing what needs to be done."

"Then what is to be done with him?" the Mother Superior asked. "The queen may stay of course but we cannot have the infant here."

There was an expectant pause as all turned to look at the midwife.

The midwife sighed.

"There's always room for one more at our table."

◇◇◇◇◇◇

"Conniving old sod," the midwife muttered to herself as she affectionately bundled up the baby.

Guinevere took Merlin's hand.

"He will be alright won't he?"

"He'll be safe," Merlin replied glancing at the midwife who was now cooing at the baby, "and loved."

"They are a good family?"

"Her husband makes barrels and their other children are grown."

Guinevere smiled hesitantly.

"Don't worry," Merlin reassured her, "I'll be keeping an eye on him and his descendants who will follow, for as long as I am needed."

Present Day

The circular chamber reeked of age. Six ancient stone columns, evenly spaced around its circumference, supported the domed roof. A torch on each cast a pale light, dimly illuminating a complex pattern marked on the stone floor. At the middle of the pattern, a fire burned in a cast iron brazier, but the chamber still looked cold. It was as though it sucked the heat out of everything. The old wooden door at the northern edge of the chamber creaked open and six cowled figures made their way in. Each figure took up a position at a column and as the last took their place, the pattern on the floor appeared to glow.

"Is it time?" the first figure asked.

"All the signs say that it is," the third figure responded.

"And the boy, is he the one?" asked the fourth.

A claw like hand appeared from beneath the fifth figures robes. It flung some powder onto the fire, which flared briefly before it turned purple. The flames twirled and began to form shapes. Lines of colour twisted and entwined with each other until they began to form a scene. The scene coalesced showing a sandy haired boy, about twelve, standing at the side of a lake.

"He is," observed the fifth. "Though the time has not yet come to pass."

The first bent closer, peering at the scene. "This place is not known to me," he said doubtfully.

"It is an ancient land and yet new," said the third.

"I would see more," said the fourth and he motioned at the flames.

The scene flickered rapidly showing a barren red desert, a tropical rainforest, a huge reef, a jagged cliff faced coastline and others in rapid succession before returning to the boy.

"Was that a giant rabbit I saw?" said the first sounding even more doubtful.

"No," said the third, "it's a..."

"Enough!" said the fifth cutting him off, "He bears the mark. He is the one."

"Then it is not too late," said the sixth. "He must be killed now."

"No!" said the second figure, the only voice that sounded female. "If he dies we will never be able to claim it for ourselves."

"But the risk," said the fourth.

"There is none," the second responded.

"Then you have a plan?" asked the third.

"Yes," the second replied confidently.

"Then our fate is in your hands," observed the first as they all turned their attention back to the image that flickered in the flames.

Chapter One

Toby Cooper scratched idly at the sword-shaped birthmark on the palm of his hand. It had been itching a lot lately. He shifted the position of the flat stone he held and curled his index finger around its edge. He pulled his arm back and, in one smooth motion, skimmed it out across the lake.

Skip, skip, skip, skip, plop.

"Four!" Toby announced to no one in particular.

He reached down and selected another.

This was not how he had been expecting to spend his time. They'd been promised two weeks full of fun things. Archery, canoeing and bush walking at the school camp and Toby had been looking forward to it for ages. Now, at day three, Toby couldn't wait to get home. It wasn't homesickness. He was pretty sure of that although if he was being strictly honest (and he usually was) there was maybe just a tinge of it at the bottom. No, it was the camp itself not living up to expectations.

Skip, skip, skip, plop.

It turned out that all the fun things were only for the chosen few, at least that's how Toby thought of them. Unfortunately, they included Stanley Maguire, the biggest bully in the school. He was also captain of the year eight Aussie Rules football team so he got away with anything as long as the team was winning, which due to Maguire's aggressive tactics, it usually did.

Skip, skip, skip, skip, plop.

No, the camp was no fun. At archery on the first afternoon his job had been to pick up the arrows that 'the chosen' had seen fit to fire into the most inaccessible spots, particularly after Maguire realised that they wouldn't have to collect them. By the time they had had their fun it was too late for anyone else to have a go.

Skip, skip, plop.

Thinking about it was making Toby angry, which made him clumsy, which made him angrier.

Plop!

He hadn't even tried skipping that one.

There had been a list pinned up to the dining hall that first night. It organised who was on dishwashing duty for the duration of the camp. Toby had taken fierce pleasure in seeing Maguire's name up there for that night.

"Sir?" It was Maguire attracting the attention of Mr Lloyd, one of their teachers and the one in charge of the camp. "Sir I can't do the washing sir. It will soften my calluses and make it harder for me to hold on to the football." He held his hands up as though they proved this.

"Good point Maguire - hadn't thought of that." Mr Lloyd turned his attention to the roster thoughtfully.

"Sir? Cooper has volunteered to take my place."

"What!" was Toby's panicked response.

"Very spirited of you Cooper." Mr Lloyd said as he amended the list.

Maguire leered maliciously at Toby as they filed in.

Toby had fumed all through dinner and had broken three dishes during the washing up.

This morning they were supposed to be making rafts. After lunch some of them would then race the rafts across the lake while the rest stayed ashore watching. As they assembled in the grass picnic area near a stony beach at the south end of the lake they were informed that: A – each team would consist of ten people, only two of whom would actually go on the raft; B – no one was to go near the beach until

9

after lunch when the rafts would be launched and; C – lunch would be sandwiches. They were stored in coolers near the picnic table and no one was to go near them until then.

Untangling ropes was Toby's job and, with the monotony of the task, it didn't take long for his frustration at the whole situation to emerge so when there was a disturbance toward the beach it came as a welcome distraction. Brook, one of the girls in 'the chosen' ran up crying that she'd lost her diamond stud earrings on the beach. Rather than being told off for being on the beach she was comforted while everyone organised to go to the beach and search. Toby had taken his chance. He'd grabbed some sandwiches out of the coolers and headed off along the path that led around the lake. He doubted he'd be missed.

He flung his final stone and headed back to the path half listening to the stones progress.

Skip, skip, skip, "Ow!"

"Ow?" Toby thought. "That can't be right."

He looked back at the lake. Ripples expanded from where the stone had landed but apart from that, it looked the same as before.

Shaking his head, he headed back to the path.

The path, according to the big map back at camp, went all the way around the lake, some sections were near the shoreline while other sections went further into the bush and there were no intersections so Toby was perplexed when he discovered one. The dilemma it posed was which way to go. His plan had been to go completely around the lake so, logically, as he'd been keeping the lake on his left he should turn left here. Happy with his deduction he pressed on but soon began to worry. The path was narrowing and surely, he thought, he should have been closer to the shoreline. Instead, there seemed to be a small hill ahead. "Just a bit further," he thought, "then I'll turn back."

The path ended.

He had come to the base of a small cliff and the path stopped dead at a large crack in it.

Only it wasn't just a crack. Toby went closer. It was wide enough for Toby to enter and it widened the further in he went.

Toby had found an entrance to a cave. A big dark, wonderfully mysterious cave.

The voice of caution battled the urge to explore. Exploration won.

Dim light filtered in from outside. Toby could just make out some vague shapes but could get no real idea of the cave's full size.

Toby had never been afraid of the dark. Of course, there was that time he'd accidentally locked himself in the supply room at school and there had been a power blackout. That had been scary. And there was the time he'd been playing late in his cubby in the backyard and his father had forgotten he was out there and turned the floodlights off just as a cat landed on the roof of the cubby. He'd torn his jeans in his panic to scramble out. There was also the time when he was little and had climbed into an empty blanket box and the lid had fallen shut. He'd cried for half an hour before anyone heard him. But, in general, he wasn't afraid of the dark.

He walked forward. Each footstep echoed in the quiet. He stopped. It was very quiet. So quiet he could hear his heart pounding in his ears. He stood still letting his eyes adjust. Detail began to emerge from the gloom. Stalactites hanging from the roof, stalagmites rising to meet them became visible creating an array of weird shapes in the faint light. One looked like a statue of a mother and child he'd seen last time they'd been on an excursion to the gallery of modern art, another looked like a Rastafarians dreadlocks. One in particular looked like an old man lying on his back on a bench.

The outcrop drew Toby. He took one step forward

then another and another and...

CRACK!!!

The sound echoed loudly around the cave and the place appeared to give a slight shudder.

Toby turned and bolted. He didn't stop until he was back on the main path where he finally allowed himself a breath as he looked back at the cave entrance. Nothing else seemed to have happened. For a moment he debated going back in but a glance at his watch changed that. Somehow he'd managed to be in that cave for three hours and it was now fast approaching evening mealtime. Without further thought, he made his way back to the camp at a run.

Chapter Two

He arrived back breathless but in time to join the rowdy throng queuing through the dining hut's doors.

After picking up a plate of sausages, some suspicious looking vegetables and some mashed potato, which was tonight's only menu option, he made his way to find a seat at the tables. Peter beckoned him over. Peter DeSilva was Toby's best friend. He was a brilliant athlete and should have been one of 'the chosen' but for one thing. He played tennis not football and so was some sort of sissy as far as they were concerned.

"Where were you?" Peter asked after Toby had settled himself down and started to eat.

"Further round the lake," Toby replied. "Did anyone notice I was gone?"

"Apart from me you mean?"

Toby nodded.

"No I don't think so." Peter said. "They were too busy trying to find Brook's precious earrings. Kept us looking all day because they were 'Oh so valuable!'" Peter snorted as he paused to shove a large forkful of mashed potato into his mouth. "Wmfff mffff.." Toby raised one eyebrow at Peter who rolled his eyes back at Toby but stopped trying to talk long enough to swallow. "We never did though."

"Shame." Toby said, not upset at all.

"Only because she wasn't wearing them to start with," Peter continued. "Found them in her bed when we finally got back."

"She in trouble?" Toby asked.

"Nah! Teachers were just pleased that she'd found them. I think they were worried about insurance or something," Peter said shrugging. "She's not as popular with everyone else though."

"Especially with those who were meant to go on the rafts?" deduced Toby.

"You got it." Peter placed a piece of sausage in his mouth and chewed for a moment before swallowing with a grimace. "Disgusting! Anyway what were you doing all day?"

"Just wandering around a bit." Toby replied noncommittally, not sure how much he wanted to share but then... "I found a cave," he added enthusiastically.

"A cave?"

"Yeah!"

"Cool!"

During the rest of the meal, Toby described the cave in as much detail as he could remember and before dinner had finished they'd formulated a plan to sneak off tomorrow and explore it together.

◇◇◇◇◇◇

The next morning they set off straight after breakfast. The morning was set aside as free time in which they where supposed to write a letter home saying how much fun they were having and how good the food was. The last bit had been emphasised by the teachers. Toby and Peter had written theirs the last night by torchlight under their blankets so as not to disturb the others who shared their cabin. They had even thought out a way to get themselves permission to leave the campsite. They approached Miss Sonnet and asked if they could write by the lake as it gave them inspiration. She gave them permission with a glisten in her eye muttering 'how poetic' to herself as they headed off.

They had only gone about halfway when they heard someone crying. Rounding a corner, they found Brook, sitting on a rock and looking miserable. Peter looked at Toby as if to say lets go back and see if we can find a way around her but before they could backtrack, she looked up.

"What do you want?"

"Nothing!" they both replied in unison.

"Then go away and leave me alone." Brook sobbed.

"Suits me." Peter stated "C'mon." and he turned to go.

"Wait."

Toby had never been fond of Brook. In fact she'd barely exchanged ten words with him and most of those had been narky snide remarks about his clothes or the fact that he wasn't on the football team but there was something inside him that couldn't let someone be this upset without wanting to help.

Toby went and sat down near Brook, ignoring Peter who was rolling his eyes and shaking his head.

"What's wrong?" Toby asked.

"As if you don't know," was the sarcastic reply.

"If it's about yesterday..."

"Yes, yes, yes! I know! If I hadn't been so stupid we'd have gone on the rafts." She stopped and looked coldly at Toby. "Not that you'd have been on one anyway."

"Fine." Toby stood. "I leave you to be comforted by your friends."

This brought on a fresh round of tears and then in a small voice. "They're not my friends are they?" Toby shrugged. "They were my grandmother's. The earrings. She left them to me. Mum said I shouldn't bring them because they might get lost and when I thought they were I...."

"But they weren't lost."

"But now everybody hates me because I ruined the raft race."

Toby shrugged. "Whole thing gave me a chance to clear off so from my point of view you did a good thing."

Brook's attitude changed completely. "You snuck off?"

"Yes. So?"

"I bet Mr Lloyd will be interested in hearing about that." She stood up, her tears miraculously gone. "And I'm sure that you're both not supposed to be out here now." With a malicious smile, she flounced off.

"Wait!" Toby called but Brook ignored him and disappeared around a corner.

"That's all I need," Peter complained. "Lloyd doesn't like me much anyway."

"She won't tell him."

"Why not?" Peter asked.

"Because she'll buy her way back in by telling Maguire so he can tell on us." Toby said.

"I don't see how it helps. We'll still be in trouble."

"No we won't"

Peter was now completely confused. "How come?"

"Because," Toby answered, "we've got permission."

Peter smiled. "So Maguire will look like an idiot and it will be Brook's fault. Neat."

Peter's mood lifted appreciably as they continued though Toby was not quite as pleased. He hadn't intended for Brook to end up worse off and he was now sure she would. He made a mental note to make it up to her when he could and set his mind to finding the path to the cave.

Peter, who had been prodding at various bushes with a stick said, "Are you sure there was a path?"

"Positive." was Toby's firm reply though, just quietly, he was beginning to have doubts. "I'll try a bit further up."

Peter nodded his assent as Toby trotted off.

They continued searching without luck for another half an hour until finally, Peter said: "That's it. I don't think there is a path."

Toby's doubts had been growing as well, but... "Let's just search a little longer," he pleaded.

"No. I'm going to head back. We've already wasted half the morning."

Toby glanced at his watch. "There's still two hours to go before lunch."

"Yeah. And I don't want to spend it wandering back and forth along this path. I'm heading back."

Toby was torn. He really wanted to find the cave.

"I'll have just one more, quick look. Then I'll catch you up."

"Suit yourself." Peter replied and without further ado headed back down the path.

Toby watched him until he disappeared around a bend before continuing his search.

Within moments the scenery started looking very familiar then, suddenly, there it was. Exactly as he'd remembered it from yesterday.

He ran back down the path to catch up to Peter and tell him but the path was empty. There was no sign of Peter at all.

Chapter Three

"Peter?" No reply. Toby went back further. "Peter?" Still no response. "PETER!!"

He must have run, Toby thought to himself, to have gotten so far so quickly.

Toby was annoyed with Peter. If only he'd stuck it out a bit longer they could have both explored the cave. Now there was only going to be him. "Oh well," he shrugged, "his loss."

With that, Toby headed down the path and in no time, it seemed he was at the entrance to the cave.

He peered into the darkness. It occurred to him at this point that next time he was planning an expedition into a cave it might be a good idea to bring a torch. Still, if memory served, there had been some dim light. Enough light, perhaps, that if he waited just inside for a bit, his eyes would adjust.

With that bit of rationalisation, Toby plunged in.

Perhaps he was imagining it but the cave seemed less gloomy than before. The feature he'd thought of as the mother and child now just looked like two rounded stalagmites, the outcrop that resembled a Rastafarian's hair still looked like dreadlocks only more tangled. And there was something else.

A movement further into the gloom caught his eye.

"I've been expecting you." The deep voice made Toby's heart miss a beat.

He turned and ran back out, stopping to calm down.

Peter! It must have been Peter, Toby thought. He must have been hiding and when Toby went back, he'd snuck down the path and into the cave waiting for Toby to come so he could play his joke.

Convinced that he was right, Toby went back in.

"Peter?" Toby called. "I know it's you."

Silence

"Scared the daylights out of me if that makes you feel better." Toby added.

"That was not my intention," came the deep reply.

"Cool voice Peter."

"I'm not Peter."

Toby's stomach knotted. "What... Who...?" He edged back toward the entrance.

"Who... who are you?" Toby stammered, edging further.

"A friend." A figure emerged from the gloom. In the dim light Toby could barely make out any detail but thought that he wore a cloak and was carrying a staff. "More light?" without waiting for a response the figure struck the base of the staff against the ground. Immediately light burst from the head of the staff.

This was too much for Toby. He ran. He ran as fast and as hard as he ever had. This time he didn't stop until he got all the way back to camp.

◇◇◇◇◇◇

After catching his breath, he went to the cabin. He was hoping to find Peter there. He'd already spotted Alexis and Graham, the other boys they shared the cabin with, sitting on the steps of the dining hut.

"So much for catching up," Peter said as he walked in. "You've missed lunch."

"What?" Toby looked at his watch. It was indeed after one o'clock. Toby sat on his bed, stunned. Once again, what seemed like minutes had turned out to be hours.

"Don't worry. I stole some fruit for you. It was the only edible part of lunch anyway," said Peter, totally misinterpreting Toby's reaction.

"Er thanks." replied Toby as he took the apple that

Peter had produced from beneath his pillow and bit into it. It was floury but better than nothing.

"So you found it then did you?" Peter asked.

Toby was about to tell Peter everything but something stopped him. Whether it was the thought that Peter wouldn't believe him or that Toby was not even sure he believed himself, he wasn't sure. He didn't want to lie to his friend but sometimes the truth was just too complicated.

"Well?" Peter insisted.

"No." Toby replied. "In fact I'm starting to think that I imagined the whole thing in the first place."

Peter shrugged. "Oh well, it was fun looking. Anyway you missed all of the excitement here."

"What excitement?"

"Brook." Peter replied with a mischievous look in his eye.

Toby munched his apple as Peter filled him in on all the details.

As predicted, Brook had passed the juicy titbit of finding Toby and Peter out of the camp straight to Maguire who lost no time in telling Mr Lloyd. Peter realised what had happened the minute Mr Lloyd found him and asked him to come to the office. Once there, he explained that, yes, they were around the lake but they had permission to be there, a fact Miss Sonnet soon confirmed. Mr Lloyd then proceeded, after much prompting from Miss Sonnet, to give Maguire a lecture about telling tales and to apologise to Peter and Toby. On asking where Toby was, Peter explained that he had been so moved by the beauty of the spot he'd stayed on after finishing his letter to write a short poem. Mr Lloyd snorted at this while Miss Sonnet had wiped away another tear.

"And now" Peter finished "Brook's on the outer completely and you my friend had better write a quick poem before anyone realises you're back."

Toby groaned. He still had half an hour before the

afternoon's bush walk and he was hoping to get something more to eat.

He looked pleadingly at Peter who, with an exaggerated sigh, plucked a brownish banana out from under his pillow and handed it to Toby.

"Thanks." said Toby gratefully.

Peter looked morosely under his pillow. "I think I'd better go and steal some more."

Toby grinned and turned his attention to finding a pen and paper.

◇◇◇◇◇◇◇

After twenty minutes, Toby gave up in disgust. All he had written was a few flowery lines about 'Sunlight, dancing on the ripples and sparkling like diamonds.' with the odd 'peace' and 'tranquillity' thrown in for good measure.

Peter burst back into the cabin, his arms loaded with fruit. "You'd better hurry. They're getting ready for the walk." He shoved the fruit under his pillow, which now bulged obscenely.

Toby ripped off the sheet of paper he'd been writing on and shoved it in his pocket. He only hoped that no one would ever have to see it.

Students formed small groups as they waited outside the main office for the walk to start. The door opened and Mr Lloyd walked out onto the veranda. His gaze scanned the group of students before coming to rest on Toby.

"Cooper? Up here."

Toby reluctantly made his way to the veranda where Mr Lloyd ushered him inside.

The office was spartan, reflecting the fact that it was only a temporary place of power. Toby was mildly surprised to see Miss Sonnet sitting beside the desk, which, apart from a few chairs, was the only piece of furniture in the room. Mr Lloyd made his way around Miss Sonnet and sat down.

"I believe, Cooper," he began, "that you were out by

the lake this morning with your friend DeSilva?"

"Yes Sir," replied Toby nervously.

"Yes." Mr Lloyd folded his arms and stared suspiciously at Toby. "I also believe you stayed out a lot longer than DeSilva on the basis you were inspired to write some poetry?"

"Err yes Sir."

"Very well, I'd like to see it."

"See what Sir?" Toby asked as innocently as possible.

"Don't try my patience Cooper. Your poem, I'd like to see your poem."

Toby thought furiously. If he showed what he had done the game was up and he, and probably Peter, would be in a lot of trouble. "Well you see Sir it's only a first draft and I'm not quite comfortable, artistically speaking, with having it read yet."

Mr Lloyd held out his hand expectantly. "I don't care." Toby reluctantly reached into his pocket and took out the piece of paper. Mr Lloyd snatched it from him.

"Just as I expected. Pure drivel." He passed the paper to Miss Sonnet who glanced at it.

"I think it shows some promise Frank," she responded after giving it a cursory read.

"What!" Mr Lloyd stared at her unbelievingly. "I only asked you here to confirm that whatever he came up with was rubbish. Not to encourage him."

"And that's why you're not an English teacher." snapped Miss Sonnet. "Because you wouldn't notice literature unless it strolled out onto a football field and kicked a goal." This outburst was totally out of character. "I think it's despicable the way you favour some pupils whilst crushing the spirit of those that you deem unfit for whatever it is you feel is worthy of your interest."

With that, she stood and stormed out. Both Toby and Mr Lloyd gaped after her. After a couple of seconds of stunned silence Mr Lloyd recovered his composure and sent Toby back out to wait with the rest.

◇◇◇◇◇◇◇

The bushwalk had been uneventful, apart from when Maguire managed to push Toby through a spider's web and Peter into a creek while making it look completely accidental. 'The chosen' had made so much noise as they blundered through the bush that they scared all the wildlife away. One boy claimed to have seen a koala at the top of one tree but it turned out only to be an old bird nest that slightly resembled the shape of a koala (but only if you squinted and didn't look properly). However, when they got back Miss Sonnet pulled him aside.

"I don't want you to have the wrong impression Toby." she began, "Mr Lloyd and I disagree on many things but he is still in charge and I shouldn't have argued with him in front of you and I would appreciate it if you did not mention it to anyone. That having been said, I am inclined to agree with his summation of what you had written." Toby's heart fell. He was going to get in trouble and would probably get Peter in trouble as well. "However," she continued, "I meant what I said. You do show some promise. I would very much like for you to write that poem properly."

That night, as they all sat on their bunks trying to digest another inedible meal, Toby relayed in detail his encounter in the office.

"She really said that?" asked Alexis, as Toby reached the climax of his story.

"Ah huh." Toby replied, plucking bits of spider web from his hair, "Mr Lloyd was furious."

"I bet." added Josh.

"But you're not to say anything," Toby went on, "because Miss Sonnet asked me not to tell anyone."

They discussed the best way to agree to this whilst managing to tell as many as possible until lights out.

Toby waited until they all were asleep. He hadn't

mentioned anything about the poetry to them out of embarrassment but at the same time, he did feel obliged to have a go at it if only because Miss Sonnet had covered for them.

He grabbed his notepad, pencil and torch and pulled the blanket over his head.

He chewed on his pencil for a while not sure what to write. The lake is what started all this, he thought. The lake... the lake... Toby went into a kind of daze and began to write

> *I look at the lake as it shimmers like silk.*
> *I watch the ripples as they sparkle in the sun.*
> *I hear the water lapping gently on the beach*
> *I sit by the shore and find tranquillity.*

With a jolt, he snapped out of it. For a good minute, he just stared at the paper, not quite comprehending what he'd done. He read it. He read it again. It almost seemed good.

Satisfied, and still slightly surprised, he copied it out neatly onto a fresh sheet, which he quietly folded and put in his jeans pocket to give to Miss Sonnet in the morning.

With that, he switched off his torch and went to sleep.

Chapter Four

Toby could not sleep. Every time he came close to drifting off his mind would fill with images of the cave and the old man. Who was he? Why was he there? And how come he'd said 'I've been expecting you? The questions just kept rolling around in Toby's head. To top it off his birthmark was itching furiously. He tossed and turned attracting the occasional curse from the others. He tried thinking of something else but everything led his mind back to the cave and the mysterious old man. Who was he? Toby had to find out.

As the predawn light filtered through the windows, Toby made his decision. He climbed out of bed and dressed quietly so as not to wake the others. Grabbing his jacket, he eased open the cabin door and went out, tiptoeing back a few moments later to grab his torch.

◇◇◇◇◇◇

The track around the lake was still in semi darkness but Toby had no trouble finding the path to the cave this time. He flicked on the torch and ventured in.

Toby cast the torch beam around the cave. There was the mother and child, there was the hair and there, sitting patiently on a rock, was an old man.

"Good, you're back." the old man said as he jumped sprightly off the rock and approached Toby. "We have much to do."

The Old Man's beard flowed almost to his waist and his sharp long nose protruded from inside the hood of his cloak. He reached up and pulled back the hood.

A shock of white hair fell out and Toby looked into

a pair of soft grey eyes that twinkled as the old man smiled.

"Well met my young friend," he said as he grabbed a startled Toby by the shoulders. "I've been waiting for you for a long time"

Toby started to back away

"Me? You've been waiting for me?"

"Yes my boy. I have been waiting here for you to arrive."

Curiosity replaced fear as Toby stepped away from the entrance.

"But how did you know I would come here?"

"I know a lot about you," the old man replied cryptically.

"Like what?" Toby demanded

"Well I know your name."

"You know that my name's Toby?"

The old man's eyebrows shot up.

"Er yes," he said, quickly covering his surprise.

"Hang on." Toby realised what he'd said and was becoming just a bit suspicious. "I think I'd better go."

"I also know," the old man pressed on, "about that birthmark on your hand and why it's been bothering you of late."

That stopped Toby in his tracks. He held his palm out toward the old man. The normally pale purple mark was an angry red.

"Who are you?"

"I have many names," the old man replied.

"Then just tell me one of them."

"Very well." The old man took a dramatic pause. "Some call me Merlin."

Toby laughed. He couldn't help it. The old man's smile evaporated.

"I have not slept on a rock for fifteen hundred years to be mocked!"

"Sorry," said Toby, still trying to suppress a grin, "But Merlin?"

"Yes?"

"As in 'the Merlin'? King Arthur's Merlin?"

"I know of no other." Merlin replied.

Toby gave him a long sceptical look. "Are you trying to say that Merlin, the great magician of King Arthur has been waiting here for fifteen hundred years for me?"

"Yes!"

"And you don't think that sounds ridiculous?"

"Not really," Merlin responded. "Seeing as you are the heir to his legacy."

"The what?" Toby exclaimed. "You must be joking!"

Merlin gathered himself up. "THIS IS NOT A MATTER ABOUT WHICH I WOULD JOKE!" Then in a quieter voice, "You are the heir of the legacy of King Arthur and your birthmark is what tells me this."

Toby looked down at his hand. "All of Arthur's descendants carry a birthmark that resembles the hilt of a sword," Merlin explained, "Your father has it, so does your grandfather and his before him. But yours is different isn't it?" Toby nodded. He'd always wondered about that. His father's and grandfather's were identical to each other and did strongly resemble a hilt. Toby's did look like theirs with one exception. His had a blade attached.

Merlin placed a hand on his shoulder. "You, my boy, are the Pendragon."

"But King Arthur was a myth. He never existed."

"What!" Merlin exclaimed. "But surely in the history books..." He gazed off into to the distance as though focusing on something unseen. "I see." he said to himself. "Very clever."

"What are you doing?"

"Hmm?" Merlin's focus returned. "Oh I was just looking out on the world. It's a small trick I picked up off a fortune-teller, quite useful really." Merlin sat on a rock and let out a deep breath. "And it seems you are right and yet wrong at the same time. Our enemies, and we have them, were quite clever. Take the truth and wrap it in a story until the truth is forgotten and then the story fades."

"Is that what happened?" Toby asked. "King Arthur was real but they made it seem like a story?"

"Yes," Merlin replied. "And they nearly succeeded, but some truths are not so easily forgotten, no matter how much story they are hidden in. Those stories become myths." He chuckled "I suspect they were not too pleased at how it turned out."

Toby had read a bit about King Arthur and had seen a couple of movies based on it all and there was one 'fact' that needed an explanation. "I didn't think he had any children with Guinevere."

"Ah. Well yes." Merlin told Toby the story of Guinevere's pregnancy and the events following the birth.

"So the barrel maker's wife took him in, my ancestor, and raised him?" Toby confirmed as Merlin finished his tale.

"Correct." Toby still looked a bit doubtful. "Have you ever considered your surname?" Merlin continued. Toby shook his head. "Many names come from the trades that people practiced such as Smith, Baker, Weaver and Cooper."

"Cooper?" Toby said in surprise. "What does a cooper do?"

"Makes barrels." said Merlin smugly as he watched Toby process this final bit of information.

It was the clincher. Belief flooded through him. He was a descendant of King Arthur. It made his head swim. There was, however one little corner of doubt.

"Just one thing," Toby said.

"Yes?" Merlin warily replied.

"You seemed surprised that my name was Toby."

"Ah that." said Merlin "Well you see according to prophecy your name should also be Arthur."

"Oh." said Toby thoughtfully and after a pause

added, "It's my middle name."

Merlin raised a quizzical eyebrow. "It was supposed to be my first name," Toby continued, "but Mum wouldn't have it. Said she'd known an Arthur in school and he was an absolute dork and she swore never to have a child with that name. They had a huge row because Dad really wanted me to be called Arthur but he couldn't give a reason so, in the end they compromised." Toby shrugged. He liked his name and personally thought Arthur sounded a bit pompous.

"Well that explains that," was Merlin's satisfied response. "Anyway down to business. You have the sword?"

"What sword?"

"The one the lady gave you," Merlin said.

"What lady?" was Toby's confused reply

"Are you saying you don't have the sword?" said Merlin as he stood up.

"I've never had any sword," Toby replied.

"Hmmm." Merlin paced up and down in deep thought. "Wait here a minute." Merlin stepped off and vanished into the gloom

He returned moments later.

"Ah yes well. Humph." He cleared his throat. "It appears," Merlin explained, "that as she was about to make an appearance, someone threw a rock at her."

"Oh!" Toby thought back to that afternoon of skipping stones. "I think that was me."

"In that case my young friend there is only one thing to do."

"And what's that?"

"Go and apologise," Merlin replied as he ushered Toby out the entrance.

Chapter Five

The sun was clear of the horizon as Toby stared out across the lake. He estimated it was getting close to breakfast time and he hoped that this wouldn't take too long because it was going to be hard to keep coming up with excuses for being late. Besides, as unappetising as it was he would like the chance to eat breakfast. He bent and picked up a stone and prepared to skip it, but dropped it again as he remembered that this is what started everything in the first place.

How was he supposed to apologise to a lake?

"I'm sorry," he yelled out at the lake.

Nothing. Toby wasn't that surprised.

"I'm very sorry!" he yelled again feeling slightly foolish.

He could just go. Head back to camp and forget all about it. Forget he was the heir to the legacy of King Arthur (whatever that meant) and get on with his life. His palm itched. Okay, so he had to find a way to make it up to whatever power it was that lived in the lake. He still wasn't clear on that bit. Merlin had tried to explain that all the lakes were connected in spirit which is why it was possible for the lady of the lake to be on the other side of the world from where the stories had her. The itch worsened. A present, if he gave it a present that just might satisfy it. The itch was becoming distracting and Toby was fighting the urge to scratch as it was already tender and if he kept scratching, it would only get worse. He shoved his hand in his pocket to remove the temptation, his eyes widened as his hand encountered a piece of paper.

"My poem," he exclaimed aloud. "Perfect."

Carefully he pulled it out and after a moment of thought folded it into a boat. Gently he placed it on the water and gave it a soft shove to send it on its way.

It drifted slowly for a metre or so but then seemed to pick up speed. In no time, it was nearing the middle of the lake. Suddenly it stopped and began to spin as though stuck in a whirlpool. It went around three times then vanished.

Toby looked vainly for a sign that this had worked but all he could see were a few bubbles where the boat had disappeared.

With a sigh, Toby sat down and began scratching his birthmark.

A few more bubbles appeared followed by a huge surge of water that spouted into the air. It settled to reveal the most beautiful woman Toby had ever seen. Her face was pale, almost ethereal, her hair long, golden and flowing, her eyes the deepest blue. She was dressed in a silver gown that shimmered as she flowed across the lake toward Toby. In her hands, she held a sword. The sword. The polished blade gleamed as it caught the sun. Toby could see his reflection in it. The sword's guard was a slightly curved crossbar narrowing slightly in the middle and flaring at either end while the leather and wood hilt was un-embellished. The only part of the sword that had any decoration was the pommel; it was a round circle with a cross in the middle. It was simple. It was beautiful. It was Excalibur.

With a flourish, she offered it to Toby.

Tentatively he placed his hand on the hilt and gasped. The fierce itching on his palm stopped the instant he touch the hilt. Toby curled his fingers around it and he took hold of it properly. Some sort of force flowed into him. Toby felt like he could do anything, be anyone. He felt he could take on all the Maguires in the world and win. He felt as if he and the sword were one.

He looked back at the lady and noticed that she held his poem in her hand. He bowed to her; it seemed the right thing to do. She smiled, putting the hand that held his poem to her heart as she took a step back and dissolved back into the lake.

Toby was left standing at the edge of the lake holding a sword and feeling slightly odd.

Not knowing what else to do he carried the sword back to the cave.

Merlin was delighted. "Excellent." he said as Toby arrived back. "Now that you have the sword we can get started, we have much to do."

Merlin began bustling round pulling books, candles, a couple of chairs and a table out from behind rocks that Toby would have sworn weren't there just before.

"Look I'm going to have to get back," Toby said as Merlin started a fire in what originally looked like a crevice but now appeared to be a full-blown fireplace.

"We have a lot of catching up to do if you are to be ready," said Merlin.

"But I'll get in trouble when they notice I'm gone," pleaded Toby

"Nonsense!" snapped Merlin. "They won't notice. Time doesn't work the same way in here."

"You're telling me! Every time I'm in here it seems hours pass outside," said Toby, rolling his eyes.

"What?" Merlin looked sharply at him.

"Ten minutes in here," explained Toby, "and I seem to lose an hour or more back at camp."

"Hmmm." Merlin stopped what he was doing and ran his hand thoughtfully through his beard. "Ah!" He went to a bowl of crystals that Toby would also have sworn wasn't there and muttered a few strange sounding phrases.

The bowl glowed briefly and Merlin nodded in satisfaction. "Fixed,." he informed Toby. "Forgot to fine tune it after I woke up."

"Oh good," said Toby half-heartedly, not quite knowing what to say.

"Yes. It means there's no need for you to leave right now."

"You mean apart from the fact that I've probably missed breakfast?" Toby said as his stomach growled.

"I have food here. I'm sure I can make us a suitable repast," Merlin opened a cupboard that had recently made itself apparent and peered inside. He recoiled immediately his face screwed up as he tried to waft fresh air up his nose. "Err perhaps not. Um why don't you return to your camp for today and come back tomorrow."

"Ok then." He made for the entrance. "What about this?" asked Toby, indicating Excalibur.

"You must take it with you," replied Merlin.

"I can't wander around carrying a sword," exclaimed Toby.

"No, of course not," replied Merlin. "How silly of me. I'm sure I've got a scabbard and belt lying around here somewhere that will fit."

"No, I mean I can't carry a sword around even if it is in a scabbard."

"But Excalibur must not leave your side," insisted Merlin. "You have to carry it."

"No one carries swords any more," Toby explained as patiently as he could, "and they haven't for hundreds of years."

"Really?" Merlin seemed surprised. "I'd better have a good look outside this time." Merlin sat in the chair by the fire. He stared into the flame and his eyes lost focus, as he appeared to go into a trance. Then he began to mutter to himself.

"Hmmm oh yes, I see. Not even knives! Well, well!" Then the muttering became unintelligible until, "Ah now that's a possibility. Let me see, yes, yes, no problem there, good, good, perfect" His eyes snapped open. "I have a solution."

"Stand over there and hold Excalibur up," he instructed.

Toby shuffled to the indicated spot and held Excalibur aloft. Merlin took his staff and muttered a few strange words. Suddenly he thrust his staff towards Toby and there was a blinding flash of light. Toby gasped as he clutched at the air previously occupied by Excalibur but the sword was gone. He looked down at his hands only to find a neck chain draped over his fingers. He lifted it up and noticed there, hanging on the end of the chain was a perfect miniature version of Excalibur.

"It's the real Excalibur," said Merlin, anticipating Toby's reaction. "I've just made it a bit more..." he paused looking for the right word.

"Discreet?" Toby offered.

"Yes, discreet," continued Merlin. "Put it on." he encouraged.

Toby placed the chain over his head and tucked Excalibur beneath his shirt, concealing it from sight.

"Excellent." Merlin clasped Toby's shoulder, "Return tomorrow morning and I will begin your instruction."

Toby wriggled his shoulders settling things in place and getting himself used to the idea that he was now wearing the most famous sword in history around his neck. "Umm okay."

"Perhaps," Merlin glanced ruefully at the cupboard, "you might be able to bring some food?

"Camp food? You'd be better off with what's in the cupboard," Toby observed dryly.

Chapter Six

It was obvious he'd missed breakfast. The dining hall was deserted, except for a couple of students helping to clear up. Toby pressed his face up to the glass in the door, hoping to catch their attention so he could try to wheedle some fruit or something.

"Missed another meal haven't we Cooper?" It was Mr Lloyd.

"Yes sir." replied Toby despondently. His stomach growled audibly.

"Why?"

Toby knew he was in for it no matter what he said so, after a moments thought, he opted for an abbreviated form of the truth.

"I went for a walk," replied Toby (true) "and I lost track of time." (Also true even if it was due to some maladjusted magic).

Mr Lloyd tapped his chin thoughtfully, obviously thinking of some form of suitable punishment.

"Very well," he began but got no further.

"Good morning." Miss Sonnet had appeared as if from nowhere.

"Morning." Mr Lloyd responded automatically.

Miss Sonnet stopped and smiled expectantly.

"I found young Cooper skulking around." Mr Lloyd felt compelled to explain. "It appears he missed breakfast and can't give a suitable account of himself."

"Oh dear."

"Claims he was out walking and lost track of time." Mr Lloyd added with a sneer.

"Easy to do, I love early morning walks but I often

lose track of time myself," observed Miss Sonnet, completely ignoring Mr Lloyd's tone. "I expect that has made you even hungrier," she said to Toby.

"Yes." he replied truthfully while trying not to smile at the look on Mr Lloyd's face.

"Well we can always ask the kitchen, Mr Lloyd. Can't have hungry students can we?"

"I guess not," Mr Lloyd replied through gritted teeth. "Come with me," he said to Toby.

Toby followed Mr Lloyd around the back of the dining hall where he knocked on a plain door.

It was opened by a large, solid woman wearing an apron.

"Mrs Tripe," he began. "This boy here missed breakfast this morning and I was wondering if there was a chance that you might be able to arrange something?"

"You know my policy on that, Mr Lloyd."

Mr Lloyd lowered his voice. "Yes but with the complaints we've been getting about the food the last thing I need is for someone to accuse us of not even feeding it to them."

Mrs Tripe narrowed her eyes thoughtfully. Finally, "Very well," then to Toby, "in you go. Let's see what we can scrape up."

'Scrape up' did not create images of substantial food, not if previous meals were anything to go by, nevertheless Toby entered the kitchen.

On his only other visit here, he had barely noticed the place, being far too angry at the time about washing dishes in Maguire's place. This time he looked about curiously. The kitchen was surprisingly clean, considering that most of the food so far had tasted like it was prepared in a cat's litter tray. The stainless steel benches gleamed, the utensils hanging above were polished. All in all it was a magnificent kitchen.

Mrs Tripe led Toby past the washing up sinks, down to the far end where the food was stored. A large steel door led to an industrial fridge and next to it, a wooden door led to the pantry. Cupboards lined one wall and Toby could see they were full of plates, bowls and cutlery. Along the other was a pair of swing doors that led into the dining hall and next to them was a single cupboard and a standard fridge. Both had a small sign on the front and, curiously, both had padlocks on them though, at the moment, the locks were open. Mrs Tripe indicated a chair at a large wooden table that occupied the middle.

"You can sit there. Plates are there," she said indicating the wall of cupboards, "and the food's there," she continued, pointing to the large pantry, "I have to check on the hall. Help yourself but don't be greedy."

"Thank you."

It was with no great hope of finding anything edible that Toby opened the door to the pantry. He looked up and down the shelves vainly for something, anything exciting. Finally, he settled on a large box of generic corn flakes. They were what Toby had had most mornings so far and even though they tasted like cardboard, they stood a fairly good chance of staying down.

He began pouring them into a bowl but stopped. There had to be some better food somewhere. It was then he remembered the cupboard with the lock.

He took a quick look through the porthole-shaped window in the door to make sure Mrs Tripe was nowhere in sight, then made a beeline for the cupboard

The sign said 'Reserved – Please see Mr Lloyd'. Toby opened the cupboard and his jaw dropped. It was chock full of food. Good quality food. There were muesli bars, fresh bread rolls, jams, spreads, biscuits, proper breakfast cereals, tins of soup and even chips and lollies. Everything you needed for a feast. The fridge was a similar story; fresh eggs, ham, cheese, fruit and vegetables, juice and soft drink. Toby's mouth was watering uncontrollably. Toby now realised why 'the chosen' never complained about the food. They weren't eating it. Mr Lloyd had his own supply especially for them.

Normally Toby would have left it at that and added this episode to the growing list of injustices that was his experience of Mr Lloyd, but Toby felt different now. Without thinking he opened a muesli bar and shoved the whole thing in his mouth. His eyes rolled back in sheer pleasure as he chewed. After swallowing, he began to shove as much as he could into his pockets and inside his jacket. Bars, lollies, biscuits, small cakes and, some fruit from the fridge. He was bulging. He shook himself to settle everything and make sure nothing was going to fall out before rearranging the cupboard to cover up what he'd taken. As an afterthought, he swapped the inner bags of cereal with the substandard one from the main pantry. He grinned as he thought of the looks on their faces the next morning. Finally, he added a splash of milk to his bowl so as to make it appear that it was leftovers, and left it on the table. He was about to sit down when he realised something was missing. 'Spoon' he thought. He'd no sooner grabbed it and sat down when the doors opened and Mrs Tripe strolled in.

"All done?" she asked, eying the bowl.

"Yes, thank you."

"Very good, just rinse the bowl and spoon and leave them in the sink," she instructed. "You can let yourself out the back when you're done."

With that, she turned her attention to other things and Toby, after doing as instructed, made a hasty exit.

◇◇◇◇◇◇

Peter, Alexis and Josh were all in the cabin as Toby waddled in. The zipper on his jacket had burst moments after leaving the kitchen. He'd frantically shoved various items wherever they would fit. Consequently, he made his way to the cabin very carefully due, in no small part, to the muesli bars that were stuck in his socks.

He unceremoniously unloaded everything on his bed, causing gasps of amazement from his roommates. They dived on the offered treats, ripping into them as though they hadn't eaten in a week (which was almost true).

"Whrr dib you gep dis stuff?" asked Alexis, spraying biscuit crumbs from his mouth as he spoke.

"Who cares!" said Peter as he devoured a small cake in two bites.

"I do," Josh added, "if it means you can get more!" He was cautiously nibbling a biscuit. He'd tried the egg and sausage for breakfast and was only just recovering the proper use of his stomach.

"Lloyd's private supplies." Toby told them, and then proceeded to give them a detailed description of the morning's events, excluding all mention of wizards, swords and ladies who lived in lakes.

"So," Peter said as Toby finished, "that brings us back to Josh's excellent question. Can we get any more?"

"I don't know." Toby said. "They were unlocked this morning, but how often that happens..." He shrugged.

"Then we need to find out" said Alexis. "Don't we?"

"Yes, but how?" Peter wanted to know.

A whistle blew, calling them to the morning's activity, which on this occasion was pottery.

"We'll think of something," shrugged Toby as they headed out.

Chapter Seven

"YOU WANT US TO DO WHAT?" Peter said in angry disbelief.

Toby had just told them of an idea he'd had as they waited outside the dining hall for lunch.

"Well how else are we going to get a chance?" explained Toby.

"But dishes? You want us to volunteer to do dishes?"

"Only so we can suss out the kitchen better," said Toby defensively

"Well I'm not that hungry," added Josh

They continued arguing in low voices until …

"What are you lot muttering about?" The sudden appearance of Brook startled them.

"Why?" Peter asked nastily. "Who do you want to tell?" none too subtly reminding her of their last encounter.

Brook bit back a reply and walked inside the hall, looking miserable.

It was only then that they realised the hall was open and they quickly made their way inside.

Once their trays were full, this time with some indescribable kind of salad, they made their way to a back table and continued their arguing. It wasn't long before they were arguing in circles - Toby in favour, Peter and Josh dead against with Alexis trying to agree with everyone.

Finally, "Well if you don't want to that's fine," said a thoroughly exasperated Toby, "I'll do it by myself."

He picked up his tray and went over to the notice-board where they'd pinned up the roster and studied the following morning, figuring that was the best time. Only one name sprang out to Toby as he scanned the roster, and that was Brook's.

Toby looked around the tables. Peter and Josh were pretending to ignore him but Alexis gave him a thumbs up, only stopping after a glare from Peter.

Then he spotted her seated all by herself in the far corner.

Toby made his way over and sat down opposite her. She looked up and seemed surprised to see who it was but that look soon turned sullen. "Come to gloat I suppose. You must be pleased that your little scheme worked."

Toby was half expecting this. "I didn't scheme to get you in trouble," he began. "You can believe that or not, I don't care, but it's the truth."

Brook's shoulders slumped. "I know. It was just..." she glanced over at the tables occupied by 'the chosen', "I don't know why I thought..." She sighed and un-enthusiastically pushed some of the food about her plate.

"Not what you're used to is it?" he said, changing the subject.

"It's dreadful. Is this what you've been eating?"

Toby nodded. "In fact that's why I came over. I need a favour."

Brook managed to look surprised and sceptical at the same time. "A favour, from me?"

"Yep." Toby decided to take a risk. He told Brook all about the cupboard and what he'd found in it. He explained how they wanted to take some of the food to share around with the rest then he told her that he was planning to do just that.

"So will you let me do your shift at tomorrow's breakfast?"

Brook thought about it for a moment "No." Toby's face fell. "I'll do it for you. It will be less suspicious."

41

"Why?" asked Toby, trying to figure out what Brook's offer really meant.

Brook sighed. "I feel bad that I tried to get you in trouble. Okay?"

"You do?"

"Yes," she replied in a tone that didn't allow any argument. "So let me make it up."

"Okay," he said, not quite believing what had just happened.

"Good."

"Fine."

They sat in silence for a bit, prodding at their meals.

"Toby?" Brook said, breaking the silence. "You wouldn't have any of that food left would you?"

It was archery again that afternoon. Everyone watched as those selected by Mr Lloyd, minus Brook this time, picked up a bow and made ready, once again, to have all the fun. The rest seem resigned to watching and picking up arrows but Toby had had enough. Anger at the unfairness of it all had been simmering but now it burst forth and before he realised what he was doing he had stormed up to Mr Lloyd and stood, confrontationally, in front of him.

"Sir," he began, "when will it be our turn?"

"What?" Mr Lloyd seemed startled by the interruption.

"They had a go the other day," Toby continued, indicating those with bows. "When do we?"

Mr Lloyd seemed at a loss, he was not used to anyone questioning his decisions. It hadn't happened before. "Er well... I decide who does what and when here Cooper."

Toby folded his arms in front of himself and looked Mr Lloyd straight in the eye. "I see."

"What do you mean by that Cooper?"

Toby wasn't sure but then it came to him. "Only that

42

before it was possible that you'd accidentally forgot, and you didn't mean it, but now I see you're being deliberately unfair."

Mr Lloyd was uncomfortably aware that they were now the centre of attention. If it had only been Toby, then there would have been no problem but there was a rising level of disquiet with the odd 'it isn't fair' and 'wait 'til my parents hear' distinct enough for Mr Lloyd to begin having some concerns. Thoughts of an official complaint started rearing like an annoyed snake. Definitely, something to avoid at all costs.

"Very well," he said as much to himself as to Toby before he addressed every one, "I forgot that some of you had already had a turn the other day so if those holding bows could put them down and the next group pick them up and stand at the firing line."

As satisfying as the dismayed look on the faces of the 'the chosen' was, Toby found the looks of excitement and joy on the rest even more so. A few even patted Toby on the back as they passed. Mr Lloyd looked livid.

"As for you Cooper," Mr Lloyd said in a low voice. "I want you back at camp."

"But..."

"NOW!" Mr Lloyd snarled.

◇◇◇◇◇◇

Toby didn't want to go back to camp. He wandered, running the confrontation over and over in his mind. It hadn't quite worked as planned, not that he'd actually planned any of it, in fact he'd no idea what had made him do any of it, apart from the fact that, at the time, it felt right. At least the rest were getting a go, so that was something.

After wandering aimlessly for a while, Toby finally took in his surroundings. Without realising it, he'd wandered back to the cave and was now standing at the entrance. He shrugged. If anyone could explain why he'd acted so out of character, it would be Merlin.

With that thought, he headed in.

◇◇◇◇◇◇◇

Fire crackled in the fireplace and seated next to it, was Merlin, apparently asleep. At least that's what the loud snores emanating from the old man would indicate.

"Morning already?" Merlin cocked one eye open. "I must have over compensated."

"Err no," said Toby, "it's only the afternoon. It's just that... I found myself here and..."

"You have questions." Merlin finished for him. "Ah the curiosity of the young mind. How quickly though it goes from wanting to know more to thinking it knows everything."

"What?"

"Never mind, never mind. Why don't you sit and tell me about it." Toby sat on the stool Merlin indicated. "I'd offer you something," he continued, "but ..."

"Oh!" Toby reached into his pocket and grabbed a muesli bar that he'd put there. "Here."

Merlin eyed it suspiciously.

"It's called a muesli bar." Toby explained. "They're really delicious."

Merlin took the bar and bit into it. "Eurgh." He made a face.

"You're supposed to unwrap it."

"Ah." Merlin turned the bar over, examining it with one eye then the other and occasionally prodding it with a finger.

Toby couldn't stand it any longer. He took the bar out of Merlin's hand, ripped the wrapper off, and handed it back.

Merlin cautiously nibbled on a corner. His eyebrows shot up. "Honey!" he exclaimed. "And oats and dried fruit and," he nibbled a bit more, "lots of other things I can't even identify." He polished the rest of the bar off.

"Now," he said, brushing the last few crumbs from

his beard, "what's on your mind?"

"Where do I start?" asked Toby, trying to sort out all the conflicting thoughts in his head.

"I find that the beginning is always a good place."

"Funny." said Toby, not amused.

"Very well, take a deep breath and close your eyes." Toby did as instructed. "Now think of something calming." Toby visualised the lake just as it was after the Lady had vanished. A small wistful smile crept onto his face. "Excellent," Merlin observed. "Now, what's on your mind?"

The image of the lake blurred in his mind and transformed into a face.

"Mr Lloyd." Toby's voice was flat.

"Tell me about this Mr Lloyd

"Okay," Toby braced himself and then began to speak. Every incident, no matter how minor poured out, culminating in the confrontation at archery that afternoon.

"Hmm, sounds as though it was about time someone stood up to him," observed Merlin as Toby finished.

"But he's a teacher." Toby said.

"And undeserving of that title by what you're saying," Merlin snapped. "Anyway as for you, you saw an injustice being done and you did something about it"

"But that sort of stuff's been going on for ages. Why now?" asked Toby. "It's because of the sword isn't it?" he continued, leaping to a conclusion. "Ever since this morning …"

"No, no, no," responded Merlin, "Excalibur isn't making you do anything. You can draw strength from it, certainly but it can't make you do anything that's not already in your heart to do."

Merlin leaned forward.

"You stood up for the others because it was the right thing to do and you will keep on doing it. It's in your nature my boy. People will look to you and you will respond."

"Okay," said Toby, not entirely convinced but willing to let it go for the time being. "But what about Brook?"

"Who?"

Toby sighed and explained the situation with Brook and how he'd, impulsively taken her into his confidence.

"Arthur was the same. He always gave people a second chance."

"So I did the right thing getting her to help?"

"Only time will tell on that but I suspect that you are a good judge of character."

"Oh!" Toby felt a bit deflated. He'd hoped that he would have gotten some definite answers, instead he was still full of uncertainties but strangely, he wasn't as worried about them.

"I'd better go," said Toby rising from the stool.

"Don't forget to come tomorrow morning. I wish to start your training then," Toby nodded his agreement and headed out, "and perhaps you could bring some more of those... muesli bars?"

"That will depend on how things go in the morning." Toby replied.

"I shall look forward to hearing about it then," he said as he nestled back in his chair and appeared to instantly fall asleep.

Chapter Eight

Breakfast the next morning was the strangest yet of the camp. 'The chosen' looked very unhappy and appeared to be complaining loudly. Meanwhile, everyone else was laughing and, most unusually, eating. It wasn't until Toby ate a mouthful of cereal that it hit him. It was delicious. He'd completely forgotten that he'd swapped the boxes the previous morning.

He lingered over breakfast as long as possible but caught no sign of Brook. He was starting to worry. Finally, he was the only one left sitting. He reluctantly made his way outside where he tried to wait as inconspicuously as possible.

After what seemed like an eternity, Brook emerged from the hall. She caught sight of him and made her way over.

Toby smiled at her in greeting before quickly getting to the point. "So what did you see?"

"You were right. The cupboard was left unlocked."

"Good. So all we need to do is…"

"But," continued Brook, cutting Toby off, "Mr Lloyd came in. When he saw the unlocked cupboard, he was furious. He made Mrs Tripe lock it while he was watching and made her promise never to leave it unlocked again without his authority."

"Why?"

"Something to do with some boxes being swapped?" Brook raised her eyebrows questioningly.

"Damn," cursed Toby, "I didn't think… now we'll never be able to get in."

"Doesn't matter," she went on. "I have an idea."

Toby was intrigued.

"What is it?"

"Okay," began Brook, "You know Patty?"

"Who doesn't?" replied Toby. Patty was the female equivalent of Maguire, captain of the netball team and a bully.

"Well I've been told that when I'm done up I look a lot like her."

"Done up?"

"You know, make-up, hair."

"Don't know why you bother with that stuff, I think you're pretty enough without it." Toby realised what he'd just said and turned bright red. Brook was likewise embarrassed.

"Err anyway," continued Brook, "once I'm done up, pretending I'm Patty, I take a fake note up to Mrs Tripe and ask her to open the cupboard." Brook smiled. "See? It should be easy."

Toby considered the idea from as many angles as he could. "You know," he said finally. "This just might work."

◇◇◇◇◇◇

In fact it did work. Brook put the plan into action during free time just before lunch. Toby waited anxiously around the corner from the kitchen door as Brook knocked and was admitted in. He spent a nervous five minutes, plucking bits of clay out of his ear that was there courtesy of Maguire during pottery that morning. Finally, she emerged staggering under the weight of several boxes. As soon as the kitchen door closed, Toby rushed to help her.

Brook was flushed with excitement. "That was... Wow."

"I can't believe how much you got." Toby said as he made a quick tally of the goods. Overall, there were seven boxes of muesli bars, three packets of biscuits and a large box of tinned fruit snacks as well as other assorted items that Brook had managed to fit in her pockets.

"She just kept piling it up." Brook shrugged, managing to drop several items in the process.

They made their way to Toby's cabin. Even with Toby sharing the load, it was still awkward. Toby edged the door open with his foot.

"I can't go in," said Brook with a slight note of panic in her voice. "Girls are not allowed to go into the boy's cabins."

"You've just helped to steal a whole bunch of food and you're worried about a rule?" Toby said incredulously.

"Does seem a bit silly." Brook shrugged - this time without spilling anything - and followed Toby in.

"Ahhhh!"

Peter's startled cry caused Brook and Toby to drop everything they were carrying. Brook's hands went immediately over her eyes as Peter, hurriedly tried to wrap a towel around his waist.

"What's SHE doing here?" Peter, dripping wet and wearing only the towel, demanded. He'd been clayed worse than Toby and had obviously decided that a shower was the only way to clean up.

"Helping with this," replied Toby as he picked up the supplies and placed them on the bed.

Peter's jaw dropped. So did his towel.

"Oh gross!" Brook's hands went back over her eyes. "I'm waiting outside."

"Well if you hadn't ....." protested Peter, but she was already outside leaving Peter no outlet for his embarrassed anger than his duffel bag, the contents of which were shortly strewn everywhere as Peter hunted for clean underwear.

"Hurry up and put some clothes on so she can come back in." said Toby impatiently.

"Why should she come back in?"

"Where do you think all this came from?"

Peter looked at the pile of goodies with dawning

comprehension.

"So your plan worked then?"

"No," replied Toby, causing Peter to raise an eyebrow, "but Brook's did."

"Then she'd better come back inside." Peter went to the door.

"Pants!" Toby warned.

"Oh yeah." Peter dressed as quickly as he could.

◇◇◇◇◇◇

The pile of food was even more impressive now that they had spread it out on Toby's bed. Toby knew that what they had done was, technically, wrong. Looking at all the food, though, Toby couldn't help but feel they'd done a good thing. They'd counted it all out and counted it again after they'd eaten as much as they could. Now it was time to figure out what to do with the rest and Toby had a firm view on that, but it was not going down too well.

"I still say we should share it out with everyone who's been eating the other rubbish." Toby said.

"So we'd be like that legendary guy, from history." Peter added.

"King Arthur," Toby added without thinking.

"No, no," said Peter dismissively, "that other guy. The one with the bow."

"Robin Hood." suggested Brook.

"That's him. We'd be like Robin Hood." Peter proclaimed. "Stealing from the rich."

"What about the giving to the poor?" asked Toby.

"Well, we're poor," argued Peter. "Particularly in the food area." Peter eyed the pile of goodies greedily. "At least we were."

"Brook?"

She sat thoughtfully for a moment. "Keep half and share the rest out."

It seemed like a fair compromise so they agreed to it without any further discussion, which only left the matter of how to share it out. That didn't take long and Toby was sure there'd be quite a few surprised people if they happened to check under their pillows tonight.

◇◇◇◇◇◇◇

Next morning the elation of the previous day soon became a distant memory as Merlin informed Toby that today they would start his schooling in what Merlin described as the "Lore of the sword."

After Toby had settled himself and Merlin had eaten a muesli bar that Toby brought for him, Merlin gave Toby a pile of manuscripts and told him to "read these and don't hesitate to ask questions."

Toby didn't. His first was, "how do I read this?" The language was strange. It was made of straight lines drawn in a variety of lengths. Toby had never seen anything like it. Merlin informed him that they were Ogham, prompting a blank look from Toby. With a sigh, Merlin explained that it was a form of Celtic writing favoured by the druids and bards. He picked the first sheet up and held it out.

It contained one word.

"Excalibur." Merlin translated and beckoned Toby to look at the second page. It was completely covered by the same script. Toby stared intently at it.

"Well?" Merlin said. Toby smiled inanely and shrugged. "You really can't read it?" Merlin seemed surprised.

"You expected me to?" asked Toby.

"Well yes!" Merlin let out a sigh, "Arthur could and I always assumed that it was because of having Excalibur that he could but it appears he must have learnt it elsewhere." Merlin picked up the manuscripts and dumped them unceremoniously on his table. "That will be all for today young Toby," he eyed the manuscripts, "I appear to have some work to do."

Toby left and, for a change, arrived back well before breakfast which gave him a chance to observe the effect of last night's 'Santa Claus' impersonation. Everyone was gathering in small groups, whispering and furtively showing each other what they had found. It was not long before he spotted Mr Lloyd randomly interrogating people with a huge frown on his face.

During breakfast, he heard raised voices coming from the kitchen just before Mr Lloyd stormed out leaving Mrs Tripe, arms folded, glaring after him.

Finally later in the day Mr Lloyd was seen berating Patsy to the extent that she was nearly in tears.

Next morning Toby divided his remaining stockpile to make it last for the rest of the camp. He didn't think there would be another chance to get any more. He grabbed today's ration and headed off.

"Wrr rr yuu grnng?"

Peter had opened a bleary eye and looked straight at him.

"For a walk" was all Toby could think of replying.

"Oh." Peter closed his eyes and fell instantly back to sleep.

Toby breathed a sigh of relief and headed off though he stopped several times, convinced that he could hear footsteps crunching on gravel behind him - but there was nothing. Figuring he was just jumpy from the near miss with Peter he pressed on.

He found Merlin as he'd left him, at his table, though now Merlin sat with bloodshot eyes, surrounded by piles of paper containing the translation of the original manuscripts.

"Sit." Merlin instructed as Toby arrived. Toby did so and Merlin placed one translation in front of him. "Read." The pages contained a brief history of Excalibur.

An order of druids forged Excalibur with the help of some spirit beings (dwarves, according to Merlin at which point Toby asked jokingly if there were seven of them. Merlin, though, in all seriousness had replied that he thought there were five involved but couldn't recall their names). They had foreseen that the Pendragon line was the best chance of creating a lasting peace, so had invested the sword with powers that would aid the bearer in whatever they did, but only if the cause were just. They had then entrusted it to a water spirit to deliver it to those of the line who were worthy.

Toby wondered aloud what had made him worthy.

Merlin raised an eyebrow, "I'm wondering that myself, particularly if you take sitting quietly and reading into consideration."

That was the only part written, as Toby described it, normally. The rest was all in verse form, which was the "bardic" tradition as Merlin described it. Bards would wander from place to place passing on news and telling stories in verse form mostly from memory. Toby figured that making it rhyme made it easier to remember but made it a lot harder to understand.

Most of the verses related stories of various ancient battles and while Toby found them interesting, Merlin skipped over these in favour of ones that mentioned Excalibur.

He seemed to pick snippets out at random. One read:

The Sleeping Sword shall be awake
When one whose mark is true
Stands beside the tranquil lake
When the knowing age is new

"I think this one is about you." Merlin informed Toby who looked at it in confusion. "The Sleeping Sword is Excalibur. The true mark is your birthmark being complete. The lake bit seems straightforward but I can't figure out the last line. 'Knowing age', I don't know what they mean there."

Toby thought about it for a moment before it occurred to him. "Computers! The internet!" it was Merlin's turn to look blank. "Information Technology, they are calling this the information age."

"Ah perfect." Merlin clapped his hands in delight. "Well reasoned young Toby."

Toby grinned at the praise.

"Now let's look at this one. It appears several times throughout these manuscripts so I am presuming it's important."

> *A gift's a thing that's always free*
> *Of obligation and demand*
> *Excalibur can never be*
> *Wrested from your hand*

The explanation for this one seemed straightforward. Excalibur was a gift given to him freely and he in turn could freely give it to someone else. But, and Merlin stressed this last point, no one could ever take it from him.

One other verse also appeared several times:

> *For those who wish to take the seat*
> *And make the crown their own*
> *Then hand and sword must truly meet*
> *And their blood be known*

This one confused even Merlin and Toby suspected it was a miss-translation. Like the one he'd read earlier that said, you shouldn't use Excalibur to eat porridge.

Through the ensuing days, Toby learned many things about Excalibur, which seemed to be Merlin's main preoccupation. Occasionally though Toby managed to sidetrack Merlin, getting him to talk about Arthur, and what he was like. It was a glimpse of something that no longer was, and Toby found it fascinating.

One thing he didn't learn though was how to stop Excalibur being a pendant and turn it back into a real sword. Toby had wanted to practice swinging it but try as he might he couldn't figure it out. Merlin had been completely evasive, merely saying that when the time was right he would know.

And despite Toby's pleading he refused to say more.

Chapter Nine

The camp itself continued much as before. Peter had quizzed Toby about his morning walks but Toby had been evasive and Peter soon stopped asking. No one else seemed to have noticed them, which suited Toby.

Most of the camp activities were uninspiring and there had been no need for confrontation as they were not deemed exciting enough by "the chosen" to warrant special attention. Then came the day they were canoeing.

The morning had been a build up to the actual canoeing that they would do in the afternoon. It began with a lecture from a guest instructor on canoe safety and was followed by videos showing what to do when capsized and how to paddle as a team.

After lunch, they all headed to the lake. As usual, 'the chosen' had made a beeline for the canoes and had launched them before anyone else had a chance. Mr Lloyd told the rest to sit down and enjoy the view. The most galling aspect of it was the canoes left empty on the beach.

Toby joined Peter sitting at the lakes edge. They watched the antics of the others out on the water for a while.

"Are you going to say something?" Peter finally asked, nodding in the direction of Mr Lloyd. This question was echoed by several others sitting nearby.

Toby sighed. He'd set himself up as de-facto leader at archery the other day and now they looked to him again. He couldn't let them down. He stood and made his way over to where Mr Lloyd was sitting, reading a book.

"Mr Lloyd?"

"What is it Cooper," Mr Lloyd snapped, closing his book.

"I was just wondering..."

"Yes, yes. You want the rest to have a go."

Toby nodded.

"And if I don't," Mr Lloyd sneered, "what then?"

Toby took a mental deep breath. He had been thinking about this on and off since the first time and had come up with a plan. "Then I will get every one of us to tell our parents when we get home that we didn't get to do anything."

Mr Lloyd snorted in derision.

"And suggest," Toby continued, "that they contact the other parents and write a joint letter to the school..."

"So?" Mr Lloyd scoffed.

"And ask for their money back." There. He'd said it. The sneer slowly left Mr Lloyds face as what Toby had said sunk in. Toby had suspected ever since discovering the cheap generic food, that there might be something funny going on with the money that all their parents had paid for this trip. Mr Lloyd's reaction seemed to confirm this was the case.

Mr Lloyd seemed to think about this for a moment. "Right Cooper, I am going to let your friends have a go but you are going to sit over there and not move for the rest of the afternoon. The closest you are going to get to a canoe is looking at everyone else having fun. If I so much as see you stand up I will be over like a shot." With that, Mr Lloyd went to the waters edge and beckoned for the canoes and their occupants to come to shore.

Toby sat and watched as the canoes pulled up to the beach. The deep anger he was feeling was mollified as he saw the look of delight on the faces of the rest as they lined up to get their life jackets before boarding the canoes. Those returning to shore however, were not so happy. Even the promise that they would go out again later did not do much to placate them. They kept casting venomous looks in Toby's direction as Mr Lloyd had made it clear that Toby was the one responsible for the changeover. Toby ignored their taunts and jibes and they soon gave up and went and sat in small groups as Mr Lloyd returned to his book, occasionally glancing up to make sure that Toby had not moved.

Maguire and his gang decided to pass the time skimming stones. This soon turned into a competition to see who could hit a canoe. After some near misses, those in the closest canoes were getting quite distressed. Mr Lloyd, engrossed as he was in his book, was completely oblivious to the activities unfolding on the lake so their cries only had the effect of amusing Maguire and his friends.

Maguire and friends threw another round of stones, one actually hitting the bow of one canoe. It was obvious that Maguire would keep going until someone was actually hurt. Toby was going to have to do something, but what? He waited until Mr Lloyd looked up to check on him and stood up casually walking towards Maguire. As he'd hoped, Mr Lloyd saw him, sprang to his feet, and headed straight for him.

Toby waited for the right moment before yelling, "Hey, Maguire watch where you're throwing."

Maguire spun around toward him. "Stuff you Cooper," he responded, flinging a rock at Toby. Toby sidestepped and the rock flew past him, narrowly missing Mr Lloyd who was nearing them. Even Mr Lloyd couldn't ignore this behaviour. He sent them back to camp. As they passed Maguire muttered, "I'll get you Cooper," before shouldering into Toby and shoving him back several paces.

Toby watched as Maguire went off toward the camp. Maguire had threatened him many times before, but this time he couldn't shrug off the feeling that Maguire really meant it.

◇◇◇◇◇◇◇

Dinner that night was Irish stew though the only thing Irish about it apart from its name was that bits of it were green. As he was trying to find some portion that was edible, Maguire came over.

"Cooper, this is for you." He thrust a note at Toby and left, but not before managing to knock Toby's glass of water into his lap.

After mopping himself up as best he could, Toby read the note. It was from Mr Lloyd instructing him to be at his office as soon as dinner finished. Toby crumpled the note and shoved in his jacket pocket, cursing. Dinner was just about over and he wasn't going to have time to change out of his now wet pants. He'd lost what little appetite he had and got up from the table. Might as well get it over with, he thought to himself, as he dumped the contents of his plate in the waste.

He made his way across the campground to the main office. A light shone out through the windows casting a faint illumination on the steps. Toby went and knocked gently on the door.

"Come in."

Mr Lloyd sat with his feet up on the desk, in the middle of a phone conversation. He put his hand over the mouthpiece and nodded toward a chair on Toby's side of the desk.

"Sit down Cooper."

Toby sat and waited for Mr Lloyd to finish his call. He spent the time looking around the room. It was no different from last time except for a pile of cardboard boxes in one corner. The top one was open and when Toby shifted slightly he could just make out what was in it. Football Jumpers, brand new ones too if the plastic wrappers were any indication.

Mr Lloyd hung up and focussed his attention on

Toby

"I'm assuming that there's a logical explanation for that," said Mr Lloyd indicating the damp patch on the front of Toby's pants. "And you haven't wet yourself in fright, at the thought of seeing me?"

"No!" said Toby indignantly.

"No, because I don't frighten you." He swung his legs off the desk and drew his chair closer. Leaning forward, his elbows on the desk, he peered intently at Toby. "Do I?"

Toby said nothing.

"All right then, what do you want?"

Toby was startled. "You wanted to see me!"

"No."

"But you sent a n..." Toby stopped. The note was a fake and he'd been set up. For what reason, he didn't know. "Never mind." He made to go.

"Stay Cooper." Now that you're here, I'd like to have a little chat."

Toby squirmed in his chair. Mr Lloyd's stare made him nervous.

"I'd like to know what your game is Cooper," Mr Lloyd continued. "You seem hell bent on annoying me at every turn. Is this some new approach to getting a spot on the football team?"

"No Sir."

"Then what?

"Nothing Sir."

"Don't nothing me boy." Mr Lloyd stood, leaning over the desk in his best intimidatory manner. "I want to know what you're up to."

Toby made a mental leap. The meals, the boxes in the corner, it all came together.

"You've been buying cheap food and spending the money on new gear for the football team."

"What?" was Mr Lloyd's startled response. "Don't be silly," he added nervously.

Toby knew he had guessed right. The panicked look

on Mr Lloyd's face all but confirmed this. Mr Lloyd stood, staring at Toby for what seemed like ages. Finally he spoke.

"I think you should leave now Cooper."

Toby nodded and stood up. He was shaking inside from the tension of standing up to a teacher.

"And I'd be careful of making any wild accusations if I were you."

"I can't think of any reason I'd need to, can you?" Toby said, trying to keep his voice as calm as possible.

"No." Mr Lloyd replied after a thoughtful pause, "No Cooper, I can't"

Toby nodded and walked out without another word. Once outside Toby let out a huge sigh of relief. It was a victory of sorts and he suspected that, for the few remaining days, everyone at camp would have a fair go.

Only a single light illuminated the area around the building leaving some sections of the path in deep shadow. As Toby walked through one of these patches he heard a rustle in the bushes. It was then he remembered. In all the tension, he'd forgotten that the whole meeting with Mr Lloyd was a set up.

In a second, he'd decided his best option was to get out of there. It wasn't cowardice. It was just common sense. In the shadows, with an unknown number of opponents, he didn't stand a chance. He ran.

"It's him." The voice belonged to Billy Hays, one of Maguire's friends, although 'Henchman' was a better description.

He managed no more than two steps before something caught at his shin and he tumbled, face first into the gravel path.

Toby scrambled to his knees. A foot to the small of his back sent him flying back onto the ground.

"Get me into trouble will you Cooper?" It was Maguire's voice this time.

He tried getting up again. A kick to his side sent him

sprawling. He rolled away from what he thought was the direction of his attackers and managed to get to his feet.

For the first time he wished that Excalibur was in his hand and not just hanging around his neck then he might stand a chance.

As he turned to face them, a fist caught him on the nose and he went down in a heap. A kick to his back followed by one to his stomach. Toby curled into a foetal ball. More comments followed such as 'Teach you a lesson', 'Don't mess with us' and 'There's more where that came from' each was punctuated by another kick. Toby couldn't tell who said what. He didn't care. Finally, a kick to the head sent him into oblivion.

Chapter Ten

Cold water dribbled down his face. Some got in his mouth making him splutter. He opened his eyes. It was blurry - dark and blurry. He brought an arm up to wipe his face. It hurt to move. He blinked a few times and things became clearer. He was in the cave. He tried sitting up but a hand on his chest held him down.

"Lie still young Toby." Merlin's voice filled Toby with relief. He was safe. Merlin held a cup to his lips and Toby took a swallow from it.

"Bleagghhh!" Toby sat bolt upright, spluttering as he tried to get the bitter taste out of his mouth. "What was that?" he demanded after wiping his mouth with his sleeve.

"A draught I made to make you better."

"Well..." he began indignantly before realising that he didn't hurt anymore. "Oh!"

"Ah, I see it's already worked." Merlin was pleased. "Now perhaps you can tell me what happened."

Toby gave him as many details as he could remember before finishing with his own question. "How did I end up here?"

"That was me, I found you." Merlin replied.

Toby was surprised. "You? Out of the cave?"

"Yes," Merlin arched an eyebrow, "I go for occasional walks."

Under the circumstances, the fact that Merlin had obviously been keeping an eye on him didn't rankle as much as it normally would. Instead he said, "I'm glad you did."

Toby gingerly felt his ribs then pulled up his shirt to examine his side. He was expecting to see bruising but there was none. He looked curiously at Merlin.

"It's a rather good draught even if I do say so myself."

Toby could do nothing but agree.

"Of course having Excalibur helped too." Merlin added.

"Helped?" Toby questioned, "How? I don't even know how to turn it back!"

"Just carrying it is enough." He explained. "It offers a level of protection to whoever has it, lessening the impact, and limiting the amount of damage that a blow does to you. If you weren't carrying Excalibur you would be beyond the help of a mere potion, no matter how well made it is."

"That's obviously a bit of knowledge we haven't covered yet," observed Toby dryly.

Merlin coughed nervously. "Well um ..."

"We were going to cover it weren't we?" asked Toby, "I mean it seems to be an important thing to know about."

"I didn't want you to get the wrong idea."

"Wrong idea?"

"That you were invulnerable."

Toby gave him an incredulous look

Merlin sighed and tried to explain. "You see, when I first told Arthur about this particular aspect of Excalibur, he immediately went out and picked several fights to see if it worked. I didn't want you to do the same thing."

"Turns out I didn't need to," said Toby, still slightly put out that Merlin had kept such a seemingly useful bit of information from him.

Merlin busied himself with the fire, stoking it and sending small sparks flying into the air.

"Still, I'm surprised you didn't use Excalibur," said Merlin. "It must have been tempting."

"I told you, I don't know how to turn it back."

"There's no trick you just have to want it and it will appear."

"But I did want it," Toby explained. "There was a point when I wished I had Excalibur."

Merlin stopped poking at the fire and looked at Toby. "And nothing happened?"

Toby shook his head. "No."

Merlin looked concerned. "But when you adopted a fighting stance and... Ah!" The realisation struck Merlin and he sat. "I forgot. You haven't had any martial training have you?"

"What?" said Toby, "You mean like Karate and Kung Fu?"

"No," he continued, "What I was referring to was the art of swordsmanship and the art of combat. I forgot that these arts are no longer practiced on a broad scale"

"They're not practiced at all are they?" said Toby.

"Not in a form or a place which we would find useful."

Toby picked up on the two key words, "we" and "useful."

"So I'm going to get some training?"

Merlin nodded, "We must somehow find a way to school you in those arts."

"If I was fully trained would they be able to do that to me again?" Toby asked referring to his attack.

"Once you are skilled, they won't," Merlin agreed "and with Excalibur in your hand you need fear no one."

Toby smiled. "Then perhaps I can dish a little bit of it back."

Merlin rounded on Toby, "NEVER threaten that." Toby was startled. This was a side of Merlin that Toby had not seen. "If revenge is what you seek then you are not the boy I thought you were and you are certainly not the Pendragon!"

Toby, stood silently, looking at his feet as what Merlin had said sunk in. "Sorry," he finally said, and he was. Merlin was right. He didn't want revenge. The momentary appeal of getting back at Maguire was replaced with the feeling that he didn't want to be like him and knowing that if he ever did succumb to the temptation of getting back at people that had hurt him then he'd be no better than Maguire. He didn't want revenge he just wanted things to be right.

"It's alright my boy. Just remember that with power comes responsibility. Something that is often forgotten." Merlin patted him on the shoulder. "You should head back. You've been here all night and you might be missed if there is no sign of you this morning."

"But what about Maguire?"

"Ignore him. Go about as if nothing has happened. That will be far more effective than if you went back ready to pick a fight."

Toby looked doubtful. How could he face Maguire knowing that he'd been beaten up by him? Merlin seemed to read this in him. "That Maguire," Merlin continued. "He expects you to be scared of him, especially after last night. But if you refuse to be intimidated by him, then you rob him of his power. Besides look at you now, no marks no bruises, nothing to even show what he did. You walking around as though nothing happened is something that he will find very annoying."

Toby liked the idea of annoying Maguire. In fact he was grinning about the idea all the way back.

Back at camp he attracted more than the usual looks from everyone as he made his way to what would be their second last breakfast.

Peter caught up to him out the front of the meal hall.

"Where were you last night?" he immediately asked.

"I'd rather not say."

"You didn't go off with Brook did you?" Peter asked

The thought startled Toby. Since the food heist he'd barely seen her and the few times he had she'd been hovering around the edge of her old group of friends. She'd barely given him a second glance, which upset Toby for reasons that he couldn't quite fathom just yet.

"No!" He replied a little more fervently than he'd intended

"Only Maguire has been going around saying he sorted you out last night."

That explained the looks. Maguire must have been bragging. Toby held his arm out and turned slowly around. "Do I look sorted?"

"Nah! So why'd he say that?"

"Well he had a bit of a go last night but..." Toby shrugged dismissively and went in to the hall.

He was nervous about seeing Maguire. His first thought had been to avoid him at all costs but now he'd decided to follow through completely with Merlin's advice. He was just finishing toast with vegemite – always a safe choice, particularly when you're not that hungry – when Maguire put in an appearance. He swaggered up to the servery area where he attracted Mrs Tripe's attention.

Toby finished up. He made a detour round some tables so as to pass closer to Maguire on his way out.

At his closest point he called out, "Morning Stanley." Maguire spun around and his jaw dropped. He was so startled he fumbled the plate of poached eggs he'd been handed and spilt them onto the floor.

"Cooper! I'll..." Toby had never seen Maguire turn quite that shade of purple before. He grinned and walked out.

As he left he could hear Peter's voice yelling across the hall. "Sorted him did you Maguire?" followed by laughter. Merlin was right. This was much more satisfying than picking a fight.

Toby decided not to push things though and generally steered clear of Maguire or made sure there was a teacher nearby for the rest of the day.

◇◇◇◇◇◇

It was the last morning of camp. After breakfast they would all pile onto buses for the trip back. Toby had done most of his packing the previous evening so he could still manage what would be his last trip to Merlin's cave.

He wasn't sure if he would ever see Merlin again. The camp was a long way from home and there was no way he could ever get there by himself. It worried him. There were still so many questions to be answered. He still didn't know how to use Excalibur or what he was supposed to do if and when he did. Merlin sensed his confusion when he arrived.

"You look troubled."

Toby frowned. "I just don't understand."

"Understand what?"

"Why me? Why now? And what am I supposed to do?"

"Because you are the Pendragon," Merlin placed a comforting hand on Toby's shoulder. "And the time was right and as for the other," Merlin shrugged, "This is only the first part of your adventure young Toby. I think this part was the sword finding you, the next will be you finding yourself and I think that has already started. As for the final purpose, it is not clear at the moment but I'm sure it will make itself known to you when the time comes."

"That's not much of an answer," observed Toby dryly.

"Well it's the best you're going to get for the moment," Merlin replied. "When next we meet..."

"But we won't!" Toby interrupted. "There's no way I can get out here to see you again."

Merlin laughed. "My dear boy, did you think I was tied to a particular time and place?" Toby nodded dumbly.

68

"Toby if I am tied to anything, it's you. If you had been on an Antarctic expedition then I would have been there. If you had been living in the heart of the Sahara desert, then that is where I would be as well. So when you return home, don't worry. I'll be nearby."

Relief flowed through Toby. He would not have to figure out his purpose alone.

"In the meantime be careful." Merlin smiled fondly at him. "Now run along or you'll miss your cart..."

"Bus." Toby corrected.

"Bus," Merlin continued, "and look for me."

"Where?"

"At a place where you find peace on your journey." Merlin replied cryptically.

"And where's that?" Toby demanded, but Merlin was gone. Vanished. So too had everything else. The furniture, the books: everything Toby had come to be familiar with in the last ten days was gone. He was left standing in a bare cave. Then it too began to waver as though out of focus until with a soft pop it disappeared and Toby was left standing on the main path with no evidence of the small path or the cave to be seen.

Only the presence of Excalibur hanging around his neck stopped Toby from thinking the whole thing had been a dream.

With a sigh, he went back to camp to finish packing.

◇◇◇◇◇◇

The buses pulled out on time and soon the bush land that surrounded the camp gave way to farms. Home was only a few hours away.

For Toby, it felt like a part of his life was over. So much had happened in the last two weeks that it did indeed seem like a lifetime. Then he remembered what Merlin had told him that even though one part of his life was finishing, a new part was starting and he was yet to discover what it held.

With that thought in his mind he succumbed to the

rocking sensation of the bus and drifted off to sleep.

◇◇◇

Chapter Eleven

The hiss of air brakes roused Toby. He rubbed his eyes, straightened himself in his seat and peered out the window of the bus. They were just pulling into the schools driveway and were heading for the front of the admin block where the bus set down and pick up area was.

Toby could see quite a few parents waiting as they pulled up. It was nearly lunchtime but there was no school that afternoon so they were getting a sort of long weekend and Toby was looking forward to getting home.

The doors opened and suddenly everyone seemed to be in the aisle trying to get out. Toby stayed seated until the aisle had cleared a bit then made his way out of the bus where he was immediately greeted by his mother who gave him a huge hug. Toby feigned embarrassment but inside was glad of his mother's display of affection. He caught sight of Peter wrapped in a similar embrace then spotted Maguire standing alone to one side.

Toby eventually disengaged himself and they went to collect his bags. He caught sight of a large man leaning against a van listening intently to a small radio and holding some small slips of paper. After a moment the man swore in disgust and screwed up the slips, throwing them to the ground as he pushed himself off the van and headed their way.

The man pushed his way through the crowd making his way towards Maguire. He greeted him with an angry cuff around the head and seemed annoyed that

Maguire didn't have his bags yet. Maguire dutifully pushed some of the others out of his way, grabbed his bag and left, receiving several cuffs to the head when he wasn't moving quickly enough.

Several parents exchanged meaningful glances as everyone else retrieved their bags and went to their cars. As Toby passed the van he glanced down at the discarded slips. They looked like the ones his father brought home when the Melbourne Cup was on but that was months away. Maguire's father must bet on other horse races, Toby thought to himself, and - judging by his reaction today - he wasn't winning.

◇◇◇◇◇◇◇

"Did you want to have lunch at the shops?" his mother asked as they headed home.

Toby shook his head. "I'd just like a sandwich at home if that's okay?"

His mother nodded her assent and within minutes they were pulling up at home. Toby's house was in a cul-de-sac in the older section of Middle Park. Though saying it was older quite gave the wrong impression. Eight years ago there had been nothing but cow paddocks and a pine plantation. Now there were shops, schools and all the other things that went with an area that now had seven thousand people living in it. Middle Park was what developers liked to call a 'planned community' implying that all other communities were unplanned.

The phone was ringing as they arrived home and Toby's mother went to answer it while Toby carried his bags upstairs. He dumped them on the bed and began sorting through what needed a wash but after a moment of thought dumped the entire contents into the laundry hamper. His unpacking done he headed down for lunch.

As he was halfway down he could hear his mother's voice. She was still on the phone. "He's only just got back Ron." He heard his mother say. Toby realised it was his father on the other end. "She must realise that this is very short notice." He heard her sigh. "Well yes, I suppose next weekend would be fine... I don't know why there's such urgency. I mean you said you can't even remember her. Yes, yes. No I'll put it in the calendar. Okay, bye." She hung up as Toby entered the kitchen

"That was your father," his Mother said as he walked in. "Apparently he's been contacted by some long lost cousin. She wanted us to come and stay this weekend but I said no. I presume that you wouldn't want to be away again so soon?"

Toby nodded. He was looking forward to sleeping in his own bed.

"I don't know what your father was thinking," she added as she busied herself with making lunch.

"So tell me how was camp?"

Toby was silent, dumbstruck, he didn't know what to say. So much had happened but he couldn't really talk about it. Not that Merlin had told him he couldn't. He hadn't needed to. Toby knew full well that no one would believe a word of it anyway. He toyed with the idea of mentioning Excalibur saying it was a souvenir perhaps but he rejected that notion as it would lead to too many questions such as: why was there a souvenir shop out in the middle of nowhere?

Finally he said the only thing he could think of: "Good."

◇◇◇◇◇◇

The topic of the long lost relative came up again over dinner that night. "She rang out of the blue and asked for me," his father explained, "To be honest I can't even remember her."

"What relation is she to you?" his mother asked

"Second or third cousin. She was a bit vague about that." He frowned. "She was at a huge family Christmas we had when I was ten. She remembered it even better then I do," he added as though convincing himself.

"Well it all seems a little odd is all I'm saying." his mother said. "Just ringing out of the blue like that. A letter would have been more appropriate." Toby's mother had some very firm ideas about etiquette. She would never just drop in on people without ringing first. She was constantly writing little thank you notes for lunches or dinners that they'd been to. Their lounge room was reserved for entertaining guests (Toby could count on one hand the number of occasions he'd actually sat in there for any length of time) and they had a dinner set that was only used for Sunday lunch.

"Well it's only for one night," his father went on. "And besides it will be nice to have a weekend away with all of us."

◇◇◇◇◇◇

Toby woke up next morning, automatically got dressed and was heading out before he remembered that he was home. He momentarily debated whether he should climb back into bed again and luxuriate in its crisp clean sheets, but decided not to. He went downstairs and made himself some breakfast. He savoured every mouthful.

"What are your plans for the day?" his mother asked. Toby was immediately on his guard. His mother never asked a question like that unless she already had his day planned out for him.

"I thought I might walk to the shops," he said as it was the first thing that came to mind.

"Very well but be home by lunch. I need to take you to replace some of the clothes you ruined while you were away so we'll have to go up to the Megaplex."

Toby couldn't recall ruining anything at the camp, mind you his mother's definition of 'ruin' could and often did include small stains and minor rips that no one would ever notice unless they went over his clothes with a magnifying glass.

"Okay." He finished up and after a final inspection

from his mother, to make sure he looked presentable; began the short walk to the local shopping centre.

◇◇◇◇◇◇

He had fully intended to go to the shops but as he walked his mind wandered and his thoughts kept turning to Excalibur, Merlin and the fact that he was descended from King Arthur and heir to his throne. Two weeks ago he had been a normal average boy but now he was part of something that spanned centuries. It was a lot to take on and he needed to talk about it if for no better reason than it helped to get it sorted in his own head. Of course the only person he could talk to about it was Merlin, so he spent the morning trying to find him instead.

The only clue he had was 'Where you find peace in your journey'. Toby had no idea what he meant. He didn't journey anywhere. Instead he searched some of the more secluded spots.

There was part of the nearby playground where bushes created a natural hideaway but there was nothing there but some empty cigarette packets. He went to look at some vacant blocks that were a bit overgrown but they'd been cleared and had concrete slabs already poured for the houses that would soon occupy them.

He went home frustrated. He knew Merlin must be somewhere but just couldn't think of any other places to look. He even tried looking behind the shed in the backyard, not that it was particularly peaceful there as the neighbours cat thought that it owned the shed and attacked anyone who dared venture near it, but he'd run out of ideas and didn't know when he'd get another chance to look. He'd be shopping with his mum all afternoon and Sundays were always reserved for a family trip somewhere. Then he would be back at school, something that took up far too much of his time in his opinion. He sighed. Merlin would just have to wait.

◇◇◇◇◇◇

It seemed that within a couple of days, school returned to its normal routine. His status as champion of the underdog vanished and the memories of the camp became distant with one notable exception. Maguire had not forgotten how Toby had stood up to him and, now they were back, he increased the level of bullying and intimidation as if to prove a point. The worst part was he got away with it so much.

Middle Park State College was one of the new types of government school. It catered for all years, prep through to senior. The campus was divided into three parts, junior, intermediate and senior but they all shared sporting facilities and the library. Generally it was a good school but it did seem to have a blind spot where sport was concerned. The year eight football team was on top of the ladder. At this stage of the season, that guaranteed them a spot in the finals and the school stood a good chance of winning its first ever trophy. It meant Maguire, as a key player and captain, was given a lot of free reign much to the despair of the rest of the year.

Several times as they were going in or out of class Maguire had muttered "I'm going to get you Cooper. The minute you're alone I'm going to get you good." Toby stuck close to his small group of friends. Even with Excalibur's protection he didn't want to take on Maguire. Thankfully Peter lived a street away from him so they could walk home together.

One thing did disappoint him and he couldn't really say why. Brook was completely ignoring him. Several times he'd approached Brook but she deliberately avoided him. The Monday after they got back, she regained her spot on the netball team and, while she was still not part of the group yet, she certainly didn't want to be seen hanging around with Toby and his friends. Toby shoved these strange feelings in the 'too hard basket' until he could figure them out.

The week dragged on. Normally he had the weekend

to look forward to but there was now this trip to this relative who Toby was to call 'Aunt Fay'. Toby's mother was now very enthusiastic about it, due in no small part to the very polite letter that had arrived Monday apologising for the unseemly haste in arranging the visit and assuring her that normally she would have sent a letter but was caught up in the excitement of catching up after so many years. Something didn't quite add up as far as Toby was concerned but, as he was not consulted about his feelings on the trip, he kept his reservations to himself.

Thursday was the first time since getting back that Toby walked home alone. Peter had been picked up by his mother to go to a special tennis coaching clinic and Toby had been getting glowered at by Maguire all afternoon. There were two ways that Toby could get home. The usual one he used with Peter had the advantage of going near the shops where they could usually find ways of spending their pocket money several times over. The other way cut through the environmental reserve and though longer, meant he could leave by the other gate and avoid any chance of an encounter with Maguire.

The reserve was a narrow strip of native vegetation that meandered around Middle Park acting as a divider between the various sections of the estate with a path in the middle to encourage people to 'enjoy nature'. At least that's what the brochure kept saying whenever they released a new section of land for sale. There were some sections that were wider than others and in these bits the surrounding trees were so thick you were completely surrounded by nature. Not even the noise of traffic filtered through there. Toby stopped at one of these and closed his eyes, enjoying the sound of trees rustling in the gentle breeze that always seemed to blow through here.

"It's about time!"

Toby nearly jumped out of his skin. He spun around.

It was Merlin.

"You frightened the life out of me," said Toby accusingly as his heart settled back to a normal rhythm.

"Well that will teach you for not keeping your guard up."

"What guard?" said Toby. "I don't have a guard."

"Yes, well that is something I am working on." Merlin ushered him along and for the first time Toby noticed that there was now a side path. Within moments Toby was back in the familiar surrounds of Merlin's cave.

"You took your time finding me." Merlin observed as he settled into his chair

"But I ... I..." Toby sputtered in indignation. "If you hadn't been so cryptic..."

"Cryptic? I thought that this was quite a peaceful place on your journey home."

Toby opened his mouth to reply but then closed it. Merlin was totally right. Toby was mentally kicking himself for not thinking of it the other day.

"Never mind, now that you have found me again we must organise our time together. Things are beginning to happen and your enemies are aware you have come into your inheritance."

"Enemies?" questioned Toby.

"Yes," replied Merlin. "The same ones that caused the downfall of Arthur. They have been waiting."

"For what?"

"A chance! A chance to get hold of Excalibur and make it their own. Consequently I must prepare you as best that I can and for that I need to spend some time with you young Toby, time that would be noticed."

"Can't you just do that time twiddle thing again?" Toby asked.

"No," Merlin replied. "It is important that I keep an eye on the real world at the moment and doing that within a time shift gives me a headache. No, we must find some time when you will not be missed. Now I believe you have things called weekends."

"Yes," Toby replied cautiously.

"Fascinating concept," Merlin muttered to himself. "Two days off every week. Anyway," he continued, "what parts of it can you spare?"

Toby thought for a moment. "Saturday morning would be okay. I can usually head off by myself for a couple of hours."

"Very good, I shall see you this Saturday."

Something niggled. "No!" he said as he remembered, "We are going away for the weekend."

"Oh! Where?"

"We're going to visit some relative." Toby filled Merlin in on the trip and added his personal reservations about this new found relative.

"Fay you say her name is?" Merlin seemed unduly alarmed "It could be... Toby, see if you can find out anything about this 'Aunt' Fay while you're there. I think your instincts are serving you well but," Merlin leaned forward, "Toby, I cannot emphasize this enough, be very, very careful on this trip."

Toby nodded. "I will."

Chapter Twelve

Shabby was the best description that Toby could think of as they drove up the gravel road to 'Aunt' Fay's house. It was a two-storey affair made of a crumbling dark brick. It had definitely seen better times.

"Oh it's gorgeous!" Toby's mother exclaimed as they pulled up at the huge double doors that were the entrance. Toby stared at his mother, wondering if there was another house somewhere that Toby couldn't see.

"Stunning!" his father added, obviously also looking at the other invisible house.

Toby briefly debated whether he should share his view of how run down and in need of repair the place was but the awed looks on his parent's faces made him decide against it.

Toby just gave them a noncommittal smile and got out of the car.

The huge doors swung open and a sharp-faced woman stepped out.

"Fay." His father greeted her.

"Delighted you could make it," she responded. "And this must be Toby," she said turning her attention to him, smiling and offering him her hand.

"Pleased to meet you," Toby replied politely, taking the proffered hand

Her hand felt cold and her smile looked predatory. Toby shivered at her touch.

She released his hand and ushered them inside.

It was as though they had walked into a different house. It was plush, well maintained and huge.

His entire house would have fit in the entrance hall alone.

A broad stairway dominated the entrance leading up to the second floor. At its base a small sallow looking boy about Toby's age stood waiting.

"This is Morton," 'Aunt' Fay introduced. "I'm sure he and Toby will get on famously."

The boy's mouth moved into what Toby assumed was an attempt at a smile but to his mind looked more like a sneer.

"Let me show you around." She stopped thoughtfully for a second. "I'm sure Toby would find a house tour rather boring, perhaps Morton could take Toby out into the gardens to play."

Toby's parents thought this a marvellous idea. Someone would take care of their bags and they would all meet for afternoon tea on the back patio a little later. Toby put a brave face on and somehow managed to look more cheerful than Morton did, though that was not particularly difficult.

◇◇◇◇◇◇◇

The gardens were huge with neatly trimmed hedges, flowerbeds and an ornamental pond complete with ducks. They looked as though they were straight out of one of the English melodramas that his mother liked to watch, where everyone was oh so polite, wore silly looking hats and clothes, bowed and curtsied to each other and didn't seem to do a lot else.

Morton led Toby straight to the pond. On the way, Toby tried to make conversation, with little success.

"So is Fay your mum?" Toby asked to break the ice.

"No," was the flat reply.

"Oh, is she .."

"I was adopted," Morton said to cut off any further questions.

"So you're not related then?" Toby persisted.

"Distantly." Morton sighed in frustration. "Look, I was adopted by her when I was four. I don't remember

81

my parents at all only that there was a car crash which killed them both and Morgiana was the only one who offered to take me in. There, are you happy?"

"Morgiana?"

"That's what I call her, okay?" Toby nodded his assent and didn't say another word until they reached the pond.

Morton picked up a stone and skimmed it out. Toby did likewise skipping just a bit further. Morton sent out another a bit further again and Toby noticed for the first time that he was left handed. Toby skimmed another stone and soon a friendly competition sprang up. After a few minutes of this, Toby felt things were safe enough to ask a few more questions.

"So do you like living here?" Toby asked.

"I don't," was the short reply.

"Then..."

"I don't live here. This is just a place we stay occasionally."

"Then..."

"What's with all the questions?" Morton snapped. He stormed off further around the pond and began hurling stones at the pond.

Toby left him alone for a few minutes before heading over toward him to apologise. Any thought of that soon disappeared. At first Toby thought Morton was still throwing stones in anger but then he realised he was deliberately aiming for some of the ducks that were paddling in the pond. So far, he'd missed but each stone sent one or two startled ducks flapping away.

As Toby approached, Morton took aim at a small group of ducks that were so close to him there was little chance of him missing.

"Hey stop that," Toby yelled impulsively. Morton ignored him and wound his arm back.

In three strides, Toby was over there. He caught Morton's wrist, stopping him in mid throw.

Morton struggled, trying to free his wrist but Toby

was stronger. He grabbed Morton's hand and prised the stone out of it. As he did so, he gasped and stared at Morton's now exposed palm. Morton had a birthmark shaped just like his.

Morton seized this opportunity to twist out of Toby's grasp and run back to the house leaving Toby gaping after him.

◇◇◇◇◇◇

No one mentioned the incident at the pond when he went back inside. Obviously, Morton hadn't said anything; however, he did manage to avoid Toby for the rest of the afternoon so he had no chance to quiz him about his birthmark, not that he expected he would have gotten an answer anyway. Instead, he spent his time sitting in the vast library, flicking idly through books and trying to sort out what it all meant.

According to the old scrolls there should only be one 'whose mark is complete' so how could Morton also have a birthmark? And if there was supposed to be two of them why hadn't Merlin said something? Or didn't he know? It didn't make any sense and after a while, Toby gave up thinking about it figuring as soon as they got back he'd find an excuse to go off and visit Merlin.

Toby's Mum arrived soon after to shoo him upstairs so he could change for dinner.

◇◇◇◇◇◇

At dinner that night they only managed to occupy one end of the dining table, it was that big.

The food, while looking delicious, tasted rather bland and Toby found he had to chew it a lot before he could bring himself to swallow. The conversation matched the food and most of it was 'Aunt' Fay asking questions about Toby, which his mother seemed to be only too pleased to answer endlessly.

About half way through the meal, 'Aunt' Fay opened a bottle of wine. She poured a glass for herself, Toby's parents and, surprisingly, Morton. She looked to Toby's parents, bottle still, poised, "Is the young man permitted a glass?"

His parents shared a conferring look. "I guess it would okay on this occasion." Toby's mother hesitantly replied.

"Excellent!" 'Aunt' Fay rose and went to the nearby sideboard returning a moment later with a glass that she had already filled. "Here we are, now, a toast, to reuniting relatives."

"To reuniting relatives," they echoed, raising their respective glasses.

Toby was dubious. Only on some special occasions, like Christmas dinner, was Toby permitted a small glass of wine; he hadn't expected this to be one of them and he didn't trust 'Aunt' Fay one little bit. His parents gave him an encouraging look so he raised his glass as well.

As the glass touched his lips, a sharp pain struck his chest, right where Excalibur rested. Toby flinched, dropping the glass and spilling the wine.

"Toby!" his mother cried, making a vain attempt to mop up the spill with a napkin.

"I'm sorry, it was an accident."

"Don't worry." 'Aunt' Fay seemed completely undisturbed by the accident. In fact, she looked curiously pleased.

After that, every time Toby looked at 'Aunt' Fay, she was staring straight at him with a predatory look on her face. It made him feel very uncomfortable and he was glad when dinner was finally over.

By then it was after nine o'clock and Toby didn't fight too much when his parents suggested that it was time for bed.

Chapter Thirteen

CREAK!

Toby awoke with his heart beating fast. It was still dark. The moon was behind clouds. There was not enough light to make out anything. He had a moment of panicked disorientation before he remembered where he was.

CREAK! Toby strained his ears. He could swear he heard someone muttering under their breath. The floor creaked again and the muttering sounded closer.

There was definitely someone in the room. Toby tried to sit up, but found himself unable to move. Some force was holding him down, tying him to the bed.

"Who's there?" Toby said, or at least that was what he tried to say but all that came out was "wwrrrrrr"

Suddenly a face appeared out of the gloom. Toby tried to cry out in fright but couldn't manage that either. All that he could do was look at the face as it loomed over him. Clouds parted outside and enough moonlight shone in to allow Toby to see.

"Where is it?" 'Aunt' Fay asked, in a low hissing voice.

Part of Toby was not surprised to find his suspicions about 'Aunt' Fay confirmed but the rest of him was terrified as she poised over him like a vulture. She wanted something from him and he suspected he knew what that was and if that was the case, there was no way he could let her get it.

"Well?"

"Wrrghhh," was all Toby could manage as he continued to struggle against his invisible bonds.

'Aunt' Fay made an exasperated sound as though she was annoyed with herself. She made an intricate hand movement then rephrased her question.

"Tell me where it is?"

"I don't …" Toby found he could speak. "I don't know what you're talking about."

SLAP!

The blow stung his cheek but not as much as he thought it should.

"Don't lie, boy!" 'Aunt' Fay's hand swung again. Another stinging slap. "The sword, where is the sword, boy?"

Now he knew. She wanted Excalibur and she wanted it so she could give it to Morton. He could carry it. He had the mark and that alone had been troubling. Now 'Aunt' Fay was trying to get Excalibur but she couldn't take it. That was the rule; you couldn't take it, it had to be given to you. Hold on to that thought, he thought to himself. Now to buy some time so he could think his way out of this.

"I… I don't have a sword." He began struggling again.

"LIAR!" She slapped him down. "I know you have it. What do you think protected you from the poison?"

"Poison?"

"In the wine silly boy," crowed 'Aunt' Fay, "it was a test." She moved her face even closer. "Now where is it?"

Toby struggled against whatever force it was that was holding him down.

"I'm not telling you," he said through gritted teeth.

SLAP! His face was really starting to hurt.

"Struggle all you want, boy, you cannot break my power." She muttered something under her breath and slowly closed her hand. Toby's chest tightened. He was having trouble breathing. She held him for a moment then flicked her fingers out. Toby could breath freely again. "You see boy, I have you completely in my power. You have no choice. You will give me the sword."

"NO I WON'T!" Toby felt a surge of strength radiating out from Excalibur. He sat up. It was as though the invisible ropes that were holding him down had broken. He brought his arms forward and pushed at 'Aunt' Fay flinging her off the bed and against the dresser with such force that both the dresser and 'Aunt' Fay crashed to the floor.

Toby tried to disentangle himself from the sheets so he could make for the door but he wasn't quick enough. 'Aunt' Fay picked herself up and dived on Toby.

"WHERE IS IT?" she screamed, ripping at Toby. He tried fighting her off but it was as though she was possessed. "You must have it. How else could you break free? It must be here. It must be." With a final wrench she ripped his pyjama top open freeing Excalibur and allowing it to hang in plain view.

She stopped, entranced by the sight of it.

"Oh very clever my old enemy, but not clever enough." She said to herself. She turned her attention to Toby. "Give it to me."

"No."

"Then I'll have to put you in so much pain that you will." She pushed Toby down and held him there with one hand. The other she brought to his face so the nail on her index finger was barely millimetres from his left eye. "Last chance."

Panic filled every part of his body. He tried to turn his head but the rest of her fingers gripped his face. She moved her finger closer to his eye.

"Well boy?"

Toby blinked but his eyelid caught on her finger and made his eye water.

He was about to give in when he heard the doorknob rattle.

'Aunt' Fay turned her head towards the door as it

opened and his parents burst in to the room. Their shapes silhouetted in the doorway

Toby used the distraction to crawl out from 'Aunt' Fay's grasp and close his pyjama top protectively around himself.

"Henry? Lights!" his mother's voice commanded.

"Got it." There was a click and the room filled with light.

"What's the matter?" his mother asked taking the scene.

"It sounded like he was having a nightmare," 'Aunt' Fay cut in. "I came to check myself."

Mrs Cooper looked at the overturned dresser.

"He was in a panic and accidentally pushed me," 'Aunt' Fay explained.

"She tried to poison me," Toby blurted out, causing his mother to raise a questioning eyebrow.

"See?" 'Aunt' Fay continued smoothly, "a nasty nightmare. That's why I came."

"Well I can take over now," his mother said firmly.

'Aunt' Fay nodded, "Of course," and made a dignified exit giving Toby's father a polite smile as she squeezed past him.

"Well?" his mother asked.

What should he say? If he told them everything would they even believe him? Part of him wanted to tell everything but another part, the part that was annoyingly sensible, said they wouldn't believe him anyway. It was that part of him that made him mumble, "It was just a nightmare."

His mother stared at him for a long time. She knew there was more but decided not to push it.

"All right, back to bed with you then," she said as she tucked him back in. She gave him a kiss on the forehead before turning to Mr Cooper. "We're leaving after breakfast. As soon as is polite."

Toby's father knew better than to protest and gave Toby a confused shrug before following his wife out the door.

Sleep eluded Toby the rest of the night and he avoided breakfast the next morning by claiming he felt a bit queasy. This was just the excuse his mother needed and soon they were packed and heading off out of the gravel driveway. Toby relaxed as they drove out of the main gate and was asleep almost before they got on the road.

◇◇◇

Chapter Fourteen

"Do you think it was a nightmare?" Toby's mother's voice penetrated the light slumber that car trips can often induce. Still drowsy, he was only half aware of his surroundings. He could tell they were still driving but couldn't tell where they were without opening his eyes, something he hadn't bothered doing yet with the thought that he might drift off again. But now his parents were talking about him and he wanted to listen.

"What else could it have been?" his father asked.

There was silence for a moment.

"I don't know Henry," his mother sounded perturbed. "Its just I've never seen him quite so..."

"But poison? Come on Janine that had to have been a nightmare."

There was another silence.

"I suppose," she responded unconvincingly. "But we really don't know anything about her..."

Toby forgot he was pretending to still be asleep. He opened his eyes and tried to sit up but his neck was stiff from sleeping awkwardly. He groaned unintentionally.

His mother turned and looked at him.

"We're about to stop for some petrol are you hungry?" enquired his mother.

"Yes," Toby replied without thinking.

His parents glanced meaningfully at each other.

"You must be feeling better then?" his father asked but with a strange tone to his voice that prompted a nudge from his mother.

"Err yes," Toby replied.

"Well..." his father began.

"Oh Henry," his mother interrupted, "You said yourself that it was a nightmare, and a bad one like that can leave anybody feeling a bit off."

His father, wisely, decided not to pursue the topic.

After a few minutes they spotted a travel centre and pulled off the highway.

Travel centres like this were popping up all over the place. Not only did they sell petrol but they also contained several different food outlets as well as having a small supermarket inside selling everything a traveller could need.

As they entered, Toby made a beeline for the global fast food outlet. Toby's mother sighed and followed him. Their healthy alternatives menu had managed to negate all her objections to eating there. She limited her objection to the observation that he was obviously feeling a lot better to which Toby just grinned and ordered a cheeseburger.

While Toby's focus had been food, his father had headed straight for the large array of brochures extolling the virtues of the area's local attractions.

Over their meal his father studied the brochures he'd collected and discussed the merits of the various scenic ways to go home. His mother said she didn't care which way they went as long as they stopped for milk before they got home. Toby just wished he'd feigned illness a little longer so they'd have gone straight there. He desperately needed to see Merlin, but there was no way now that he could prevent his father from exploring.

He took a bite out of his burger and resigned himself to spending a good part of the afternoon looking at bushes trimmed in such a way as to resemble various prime ministers.

They finally arrived home late in the afternoon. Toby had watched the shadows lengthen during the last part of the trip and he knew there was no chance that he'd get to slip away now that it was so late.

As they unloaded the car his mother stopped. "Milk!" she exclaimed.

"What?" his father responded.

"I forgot to get you to stop for milk, we don't have any."

Toby seized his chance. "I'll go," he volunteered.

The main shops would be shut but there was a convenience store about a ten minute walk in the other direction. "It's getting dark," she observed in a worried tone.

"He'll be fine," his father chipped in, "It's not that far and it's not as if he'll be wandering the back streets."

She looked doubtful but gave in and handed Toby some money. "If you're not back in half an hour ..." Toby grinned and disappeared out the driveway before his mother could finish her caution.

◇◇◇◇◇◇

He waited until he was around the corner before he broke into a run. Toby figured he'd have a good five minutes with Merlin and still make it to the shop and back in time. He had gone in the opposite direction from the one he would normally take to get to the reserve but with his mother watching him leave he had no choice. He cut down the next street and through an easement and soon found his way to the reserve track. He stopped to get his bearings. He hadn't been along it this late before and in the fading light it looked a lot different. He slowed his pace. The gloom was deepening and it was getting harder to see the path.

He was puffed as he arrived at the spot. Or at least he assumed it was the spot. It was getting increasingly harder to see; particularly now he was in the thicker part of the reserve.

"Merlin!" he called out. He was taking a bit of a chance but thought it unlikely that anyone was in close earshot. He called again, "Merlin!" There was no reply. He searched the bush and soon found the short path leading to the cave. Within moments he was inside. "Merlin?" his call echoed through the cave but there was no response. He waited a minute and called again. Nothing!

Toby glanced at his watch. He'd been gone fifteen minutes. He couldn't afford any more time. Cursing silently to himself, he ran out of the cave and sprinted up the track hoping that he wouldn't trip on something in the shadows. Within minutes he was out of the reserve and back amongst the houses of the estate. The streetlights had come on and so he sped up, arriving at the shop with only seven minutes to spare.

He bought the milk and ran home, walking past the last couple of houses to allow his breathing to slow and his heart to stop pounding.

He'd made it in time but the whole trip had been a waste. He hadn't found Merlin. Maybe if he left for school early tomorrow morning he might be able to speak to him but that didn't help him now. He sighed. He would just have to wait until tomorrow to tell Merlin.

◇◇◇◇◇◇

The phone rang during dinner. His mother went to answer it and returned a few moments later with an odd expression on her face.

"It's Fay," she said. "She wants to speak to Toby."

Toby gave a puzzled shrug at his parents questioning look and went out to the phone.

He cautiously picked up the receiver and put it to his ear. "Hello?"

"I want it!" 'Aunt' Fay said without preamble, "Give it to me and I'll leave you and your family in peace."

"No!" Toby said automatically.

"You have no idea what powers you are meddling with, boy," said 'Aunt' Fay.

"I know that you are evil," replied Toby.

"Is that what the old fool is telling you?" 'Aunt' Fay's

laugh was almost a cackle.

"No," Toby responded, "I pretty much figured that out myself."

There was a cold silence on the other end.

Finally…"You've had your chance boy, don't say you weren't warned because one way or another you will lose the sword!" and with that she hung up.

Toby slowly replaced the receiver, his stomach in a knot. A small part of him speculated about how easy it would be to just give her Excalibur and make all his problems go away but the rest of him knew that this was no answer. His instincts knew it would be a bad thing for them to get hold of Excalibur and he trusted his instincts.

He took a couple of deep breaths to calm himself and went back into the kitchen

"What did she want?" his father asked as he returned to the table.

"Oh err, just to see if I was feeling better." Toby replied.

"Well that was nice of her," his mother said but didn't sound sincere. "You'd better finish while it's still hot," she continued indicating Toby's meal.

Toby nodded and tried to eat but only managed a few mouthfuls. His appetite had been driven away by the confrontation on the phone.

He excused himself claiming tiredness and went upstairs to shower and get himself ready for bed. It was still early but Toby wanted the day, the weekend to be over and the best way he knew to achieve that was to go to sleep.

◇◇◇◇◇◇◇

He lay in bed, his mind whirling with images, reliving the events of yesterday and the strange boy with the birthmark like his. He needed to tell Merlin about him.

And then there was last night. Had it only been last night? She'd tried to poison him as a test. What kind of person would do that? And how had she held him down when she came into his room and how had he broken free? He needed to tell Merlin about that too.

Then there was the phone call and the implied threat. 'You and your family...' she'd said. Toby hadn't thought his parents would be involved or in danger for that matter. In fact things had been happening so quickly that he hadn't given it much thought at all. He didn't want his parents involved, didn't want to risk them. But surely Merlin would have said something if they were at risk. But what about the "...one way or another you will lose the sword!" The lore he had studied so far said they couldn't take it but 'Aunt' Fay was implying they could. That was another thing he needed to tell Merlin.

Merlin! Every direction his mind went it ended up with the same thought. He needed to speak to Merlin.

And where was Merlin? Just when he really needed to speak to him he wasn't there. The cave had been empty but not as empty as the first time. Perhaps Merlin had been there but was out the back somewhere. Or worse, perhaps they'd got to him and Toby wouldn't ever see him again. And that thought led to a multitude of things that he needed to speak to Merlin about.

Eventually, exhaustion won and Toby fell into a restless sleep.

Chapter Fifteen

Toby awoke next morning still tired. He looked across at his clock and sat bolt upright in panic. It was eight o'clock. He'd overslept. He must have forgotten to turn his alarm back on last night. He flung his bedcovers off, put on his school uniform and got ready, skipping as many steps as he thought he'd get away with.

Breakfast consisted of a swig of juice out of the bottle (causing a frown from his mum) and two slices of toast that he could eat on the way to school. He grabbed his cut lunch and was out of the door in record time.

Any thoughts he had of seeing Merlin before school had long vanished. He'd briefly entertained the idea of skipping school but the thought of doing something that out of character didn't last long. Now he was more concerned with getting to school on time and avoiding any chance of a detention after school. He'd had detention twice before - once for something he hadn't even done - and hadn't enjoyed it one little bit, so avoiding it was a very big incentive.

As he ran along the school's street he could still see other students in the playground. I'm going to make it, he thought then the faint sound of the school bell reached his ears.

He increased his pace until he was sprinting as fast as he could.

The bell finished ringing just as he reached the school gates. He pelted through them and headed across the now empty playground toward the classrooms, hoping he wouldn't be seen.

"Cooper!" His name, yelled out loudly in an

authoritative voice, was impossible to ignore. He eased up and came to a stop just past the climbing bars, panting. "Wait right there!" The voice yelled again and Toby saw the figure of a teacher coming out of the main block but couldn't make out who it was. Toby sighed inwardly. He wasn't all that late and if he was lucky he might be able to talk his way out of it but that depended on who the voice belonged to. However, luck was not running with him this morning. The teacher came closer and Toby groaned as he recognised Mr Lloyd.

Toby had managed to avoid him the first week back but now he was caught, late for school, by the one teacher who'd be the least likely to give him any leeway. The possibility of a detention increased with every step closer Mr Lloyd took.

"Well Cooper," Mr Lloyd began as he strode up to Toby and pulled a little notebook from his pocket, "No doubt you have some very good excuse for arriving after the bell."

It was a statement not a question but Toby wanted to answer it anyway. He was cut off before he could even get enough breath to say anything.

"I don't want to hear it," continued Mr Lloyd, "I've caught you and you are going to spend an hour after school contemplating things in detention."

"But..."

"I said I don't want to hear it Cooper. The office will contact your parents and let them know you'll be late tonight," he said as he finished making notes and snapped his notebook shut, "Now get to class."

Toby trudged slowly to his class. There was now no chance of seeing Merlin today. He would have to go straight home after the detention and face his mother who would be waiting, arms folded, with an expression of disbelief on her face that no amount of explanation could shift.

◇◇◇◇◇◇◇

The rest of the day was just a blur. Toby couldn't concentrate on anything. In one class he had to be asked three times before he even realised he was being spoken to. Toby suspected that if he hadn't already got detention he certainly would have had one by now.

The situation wasn't improved by Maguire. Emboldened by a win on the weekend, to which he had contributed six goals, Maguire was almost out of control. The win put the school into the finals and Mr Lloyd had already persuaded the school to purchase a trophy cabinet in anticipation. Consequently Maguire was almost untouchable.

At morning recess Toby had discovered Maguire, crouched down, brazenly going through everyone's bags and taking out whatever food he fancied. He must have been feeding quite a few people going by the pile of snacks he had already accumulated. Several year sixes were crying because not only had he taken their snacks but had quite vindictively mashed up what he didn't want into an inedible pulp. Toby stormed down the corridor yelling.

"Leave the bags alone Maguire!" He was so loud he startled the year sixes and even made Maguire jump for a moment.

"Clear off Cooper," he said as he quickly recovered his composure and continued rifling through the bags.

"I said leave them alone!" Toby did something then that, if he'd thought about it even for a second, he'd never normally have done. He gave Maguire a shove.

Maguire lost his balance and sprawled onto the pile of bags. He quickly scrambled back to his feet, his face a mask of fury.

Maguire lashed out with a kick that connected solidly with Toby's shin. It hurt. It should have hurt more. Excalibur was obviously protecting him. It meant he could keep focused so he knew what was coming next and managed to dodge the punch aimed at his nose but wasn't quick enough to avoid the punch to his stomach. He doubled over but, unlike other times, he wasn't winded. He straightened and stared Maguire right in the eye. Maguire was taken aback, normally that combination had whoever his victim was writhing on the ground. He wasn't used to them standing back up and staring him down. Still, Maguire was not one to change a plan just because it didn't appear to work. He swung another kick at Toby just as Mr Lloyd came around the corner.

"What's going on here?" Mr Lloyd asked as he took in the situation. "Are you picking fights now Cooper? One detention not enough for you?"

A small crowd was gathering behind Mr Lloyd. Some people seem to have an inbuilt radar when it comes to things that are of no concern to them. They pick up on them and manage to be there, watching, almost before anything happens

"But..." The sheer unfairness of Mr Lloyd's assessment left Toby speechless.

"Another detention might be in order," said Mr Lloyd, thoroughly enjoying himself, "in fact I think this might warrant a week's worth."

A couple of the year sixes piped up. They had seen someone stand up to Maguire and were feeling particularly brave, especially now that there were others there. "But Sir..." they said almost in unison

Mr Lloyd appeared to notice them for the first time. "What?"

They began to babble out an explanation of what actually happened but he cut them off.

"Never mind." He cursed under his breath. There was no way he could blame Cooper for the disturbance now. Not with witnesses. He thought furiously for a moment. "All right, I won't make a big deal of this. Cooper, I want you to apologize to Stanley and we'll leave it at that."

Toby was dumbfounded. Him apologize? Still, if it meant avoiding a long and messy explanation with the principal to avoid detention then it was probably worth it.

With all the self control he could muster he held out his hand and said: "I'm sorry Stanley."

Maguire was thoroughly enjoying Toby's discomfort. He took the outstretched hand and squeezed it as hard as he could. "That's all right," he replied.

Toby winced slightly as Maguire continued to crush his hand but didn't let go. Maguire was so focused on squeezing that he didn't notice the year sixes reclaiming their snacks from the pile Maguire had accumulated. Toby waited until the last of them had done so before wrenching his hand away.

"Very good," said Mr Lloyd. "Now both of you head in opposite directions."

Maguire bent down to pick up the snacks he had stolen and noticed for the first time they were gone. He wasn't happy, but even with a teacher as sympathetic to him as Mr Lloyd was, there was nothing he could really do about it. He stood back up glowering at Toby and muttered low enough that only Toby could hear: "I'll get you for this Cooper," before shouldering past Toby and heading up the corridor.

The rest of the day was uneventful, as was detention. He had to write out a thousand times, 'I will not be late for school' and after he was finished he was allowed to leave. He was slightly concerned that Maguire would be waiting for him, but he couldn't imagine him hanging around school any longer than necessary.

He trudged home uneventfully. Surprisingly his mother wasn't angry. Once he'd explained that he only had detention for being late and nothing else, she merely said that perhaps he should double check his alarm or she would start coming in and waking him; something she hadn't had to do for years. She also said she wanted him home promptly for the rest of the week.

That night he took his mother's advice and checked

and double checked his alarm. It had been a frustrating day. He could only hope tomorrow would be better.

Chapter Sixteen

Maguire was keeping a lower profile today. Some of the other teachers had got wind of what he was up to yesterday and Toby had spotted Mr Lloyd trying to explain his handling of the situation to them. Consequently there always seemed to be a teacher hovering near wherever Maguire happened to be. To say he wasn't happy about it would be an understatement. He bailed Toby up as they entered class just after lunch. Once Maguire discovered their teacher hadn't arrived yet he grabbed Toby's shirt and slammed him against the wall. Toby's heart was pounding but outwardly he gave no sign he was intimidated. He didn't want to give Maguire that satisfaction.

Maguire leaned in closer. "After school, when there are no teachers,' he sneered. "You're gonna get it." He released Toby's shirt and headed to his usual spot at the back of the classroom.

Toby spent the rest of the afternoon thinking up ways to avoid a confrontation. If he walked home with Peter as normal he'd be safe until he reached the point where they normally split up. If he went straight to Merlin he'd be vulnerable the minute he got past the school grounds. There was always the main gate on the other side of the school. He'd used it once or twice when going to Alex's place after school. If he could only get to it without Maguire and his friends seeing which way he went then he would be safe. He could find his way to the reserve track and get to Merlin from there. Now he had a plan in place, vague as it was, all he could do was wait for the school day to end.

Peter was surprised when Toby said he wouldn't be going home the normal way that afternoon particularly after Peter mentioned that the games shop had one of the new video game consoles set up and you were allowed to play it. Toby was torn but the need to see Merlin far outweighed the desire to play the latest video game. Peter didn't mention it again but kept giving him odd glances throughout the rest of the afternoon.

The bell rang signalling the end of last period. Toby waited at his desk until the room had almost cleared, then made his way to the door. He checked the corridor. It was clear but he could see Maguire and co. waiting just past the double doors at the end of it. Their attention was firmly fixed on Toby as he left the classroom so he went in the opposite direction towards the library. Maguire's eyes narrowed but he stayed put until Toby made a run for the door opposite the library entrance.

Maguire nudged the others and they ran up the corridor to catch up.

The doors Toby ran out of led to a semi courtyard. One side was bordered by the doors leading to the library that Toby had just come out; to his left was a garden while straight ahead led to the main gate out of school. But to his right was the main admin block and it was through these doors Toby quickly made his way.

He'd just closed the door behind him when Maguire and his cohorts ran out. Toby watched them through the glass panel in the door. He was counting on the fact that it would never occur to them to go into the admin block voluntarily. They looked around for a second then raced up the path to the main gate. Moments later they were back looking very unhappy. They milled around for a minute before heading back through the doors and disappearing from sight. Toby breathed a sigh of relief and spent the next few minutes reading the notice board.

Apart from the fact there was going to be a "Casual for a Cause" uniform free dress day on Thursday to raise money for Africa, there was little to interest him but it gave him a legitimate reason for staying there long enough to ensure the coast was clear. After a couple of minutes he was starting to attract the attention of some of the office staff. They weren't used to students paying that much attention to the notice board. Toby gave them a smile and left the building then headed out of the main gate. There was no sign of Maguire. His plan had worked.

◇◇◇◇◇◇

It had only taken a few minutes longer to arrive at the clearing coming as he had from the other side of the school, but he'd had to wait a moment before trying to enter the cave as there was an old man walking his dog. The dog decided this was a perfect location for a bit of personal business and Toby had to stand around waiting under the watchful glare of the old man who was sure he was up to no good. The dog finished and the man led him off muttering under his breath about the youth of today but not bothering at all about the mess his dog had left in the middle of the path.

The moment they were out of sight Toby located the cave entrance and went in. There was a fire burning cheerfully in the fireplace. There was a half full goblet of mulled wine sitting on the table. What there wasn't though was any sign of Merlin. He called out. He called out again and again. Each call more desperate. His level of panic rising each time there was no reply. He was nearly in tears. He needed to speak to Merlin. There were so many things, 'Aunt' Fay, his cousin with the birth mark, the attack. He took a few deep breaths to calm down. Okay so Merlin wasn't here. So what could he do? He couldn't talk to him but... he looked around and spied a pile of blank parchment. A note! He could leave Merlin a note.

He scrounged around and soon found a quill and

some ink. He had watched Merlin use these and it didn't look that difficult.

He straightened out a piece of parchment, dipped the quill in the ink and began to write. He only managed a large blob of ink that vaguely resembled a bear or maybe an elephant but certainly not the M he'd been trying for. He tried again and managed another large blob.

After five minutes of trying and several sheets of parchment, he hadn't even managed to write Merlin, at the start of the note.

There must be another way, he thought to himself then slapped himself on the forehead for being so stupid. He had his school bag with him. He opened it, ripped a sheet of paper out of his folder and grabbed a pen.

Now he could start,

Merlin, he wrote, I... and then he didn't know how to start. He chewed the end of his pen as he tried to think of the best way to describe what had happened. He was so lost in thought that he didn't notice there was someone else in the cave until a hand landed on his shoulder.

"Arhhh!" Toby jumped out of the seat in fright and spun around only to find Merlin standing there chuckling.

"That, young Toby," Merlin said with a smile, "will teach you to be more alert no matter how safe you feel." He looked over at the table. "It may also teach you not to waste parchment."

"Merlin!" Toby was so relieved he greeted the surprised wizard with a hug.

Merlin, not knowing what else to do, gave Toby a tentative pat on the back before extricating himself from Toby. "I gather you are pleased to see me," he observed dryly.

"You don't know the half of it," Toby said.

"Then you'd better tell me the rest," Merlin said as

he settled himself into his chair by the fire.

◇◇◇◇◇◇

Fifteen minutes later Toby was still talking. Merlin was on his third refill of mulled wine. He hadn't actually drunk any of them; they'd all been spilt as Merlin had slammed down his goblet in anger at various stages of Toby's story.

"There is much here that concerns me." Merlin said as Toby finished. "I hadn't expected Morgiana to show her hand so openly."

"Morgiana?" queried Toby then he remembered that is what Morton had called her.

"The one who calls herself 'Aunt' Fay," replied Merlin.

"So she's not a relative then?" Toby asked.

"She was telling the truth there," said Merlin. "But only as much truth as to persuade you to listen to her lies."

Toby frowned in confusion as Merlin tried to explain.

"She is definitely related to you but not closely," Merlin continued. "She's Arthur's half sister."

Toby took a moment to digest this. "That means she's sixteen hundred years old"

"Indeed!"

"She doesn't look it," Toby observed.

"I'm sure she'd be pleased to hear it," said Merlin dryly.

"But what about Morton?" Toby asked. "He's got a birthmark, exactly like mine!"

Merlin leaned back in his chair, a frown crossing his face. "I don't know Toby. You are the only heir of Pendragon I know of. He is an unknown and this concerns me. But whoever he is, he does have the mark and I suspect they were grooming him to claim Excalibur for their own purposes."

"Is that what she meant when she said I would lose the sword?" Toby asked. "She can't just take it, can she? I thought that's what it said in the scrolls?"

Merlin ran his fingers through his beard thoughtfully. "You are correct, they cannot take Excalibur from you but they may make others take it on their behalf."

"Others?" Toby asked.

"Yes," Merlin explained. "Others like that boy, Maguire, who seems to feature so prominently in all your tales. He would be a prime candidate."

"But if they did take it they couldn't use it, could they?" Toby asked.

"No," replied Merlin. "Even with this boy they couldn't use it if it was not given freely but even denying you the sword would suit them almost as well I think."

"Why?"

"Because then you could not do what you are supposed to do," Merlin replied.

"And just what am I supposed to do?" Toby asked.

Merlin stopped for a moment, as though startled by such a direct question.

"That is not yet clear," Merlin said hesitantly. "Things are happening quicker than I anticipated," he continued with more conviction; "and I must make preparations." Merlin placed both hands on Toby's shoulder. "Go now but do not worry. The next part of your journey is about to begin."

Chapter Seventeen

Toby dreaded the next day, but he needn't have. He'd spent the night pondering Merlin's words. As usual he'd left Merlin with more questions than answers and was hoping the 'journey' would begin right now and involve going far away so he could find out more with the added bonus that he wouldn't have to face Maguire at school.

Eluding him after school like that would only have made him angrier but, as it happened, when Toby arrived at school the following morning he discovered that Maguire was away sick and his cohorts kept their distance as their level of bravado was directly proportional to how close they were to Maguire.

For Toby the day was almost leisurely and the walk home was one of the few times he wasn't craning his neck around to make sure that Maguire wasn't hanging around. He made a point of going to the games shop with Peter - to make up for the previous day - but the place was so crowded with other kids trying to have a go at the new game that they gave up.

The next morning Toby remembered it was 'casual for a cause' day. He cheerfully left his uniform in a pile on the floor and pulled on jeans and a t-shirt. He scrounged around to find a dollar coin for the donation and, after a quick breakfast, headed off to school. With any luck Maguire would still be away and the day would a pleasant one like yesterday.

That hope was shattered at the school gate. Maguire was standing there extracting the gold coin donation from every student in casual dress. He was even getting those who had chosen to stay in uniform to hand over whatever money they had to him. If World Vision had Maguire on their fundraising staff and they could get him to hand the money he raised over then they could probably solve the world's problems in a week.

Toby held back slightly, waiting until Maguire was occupied with several other students, before slipping through the gate.

"Hey Cooper!" Maguire made a grab at Toby as he went past.

"I'm giving at the office, my mum needs a receipt." Toby said as he ducked under Maguire's grasp and made a run for the admin block.

Maguire pursued for a few paces until he realised that a pile of other students had taken the opportunity to get past the gate. He stopped as though to head back but the thought of getting Toby was too much and he decided to continue his pursuit. By then Toby had a good head start so all that Maguire could do was yell after him. "You're a coward, Cooper"

Toby soon reached the refuge of the admin block where he put his donation into the box provided, provoking a smile from Mrs Escritoire, the schools registrar, who organised these fundraising events. He casually mentioned what a good job Maguire was doing collecting the donations at the gate before heading off to his first class.

Toby was at class so early he was already seated when Mr Sumner, their maths teacher arrived. He gave Toby a puzzled look, no doubt confused by the sight of a student early for one of his classes, before chalking a half a dozen equations up on the board. Toby just smiled back and began copying them down.

Maguire arrived just after the bell attracting a frown from Mr Sumner, who had definite opinions about students being late. Even Maguire wasn't immune from Mr Sumner who had little or no interest in football and would cheerfully give Maguire a detention if it was warranted. Maguire apologised and went to his seat mouthing something unintelligible but obviously unpleasant at Toby as he made his way past.

Halfway through the class the PA crackled to life and the scratchy distorted voice of Mrs Escritoire asked Stanley Maguire to please come to the administration block immediately.

He returned ten minutes later looking furious. He glared at Toby and if Mr Sumner hadn't been watching, Toby thought he might have even started a fight right there in the class.

It turned out that Maguire, after initially denying everything, had been asked to empty his pockets. After discovering an exceptionally large number of one and two dollar coins he'd admitted to collecting them but had claimed that he'd merely forgotten to hand them in.

Mrs Escritoire had thanked him for his efforts and given him detention that afternoon with Mr Lloyd to help him improve his memory.

Toby stayed within sight of a teacher for the rest of the day, denying Maguire any chance of seeking revenge. Toby knew he was building up to major confrontation with Maguire but he just wasn't ready to face him. It wasn't cowardice he told himself, it was common sense. If Toby stood up to him now, no matter how noble the cause he would be beaten to a pulp.

Finally the bell sounded at the end of the day and Toby and Peter set off towards the shops hoping to get a go on the new games console.

They were distracted by the beep of a car horn. It was Peter's mum.

"They've arranged an extra practice for tonight," she said as she pulled up next to them.

"But..." Peter protested.

"Just get in," his mother said. "I've got your gear already."

With an apologetic smile Peter hopped in and they

drove off leaving Toby alone.

Toby was now at a loose end. He wasn't expected home as he'd mentioned he was going to the shop with Peter on the way. With nothing better to do (the thought of going home and catching up on his homework never crossed his mind) he headed to the shopping centre anyway.

The games place was packed with kids from several schools all crowding around the new games console. The store staff darted nervously around the edges making sure nobody left the store with anything they hadn't paid for. Toby stopped outside the store. He didn't have the enthusiasm to fight his way through to have a go. Some things were not as much fun when you were by yourself and this was something he wanted to share. He wouldn't be able to look Peter in the eye if he'd had a go on it before him. Instead he spent a half hour wandering aimlessly around the shops before deciding he may as well go home.

He headed out of the centre and up the main road. He was about halfway home when something made him look over his shoulder.

He wasn't as alone as he thought.

"Cooper!"

The yell came from Maguire who was about a hundred metres behind him and he wasn't alone. His 'friends' Billy and Warren were at their usual position on either side of him. What was he doing here? Toby thought, he was supposed to be in detention.

Toby then remembered that Mr Lloyd was in charge of detentions this week. He had obviously let Maguire off early. Toby didn't know if Maguire had had his 'friends' follow Toby or whether it was just a coincidence that Maguire was here now. It didn't matter. All that did was that Maguire was here and he was going to take revenge on Toby.

Toby weighed his options, turned and ran.

"Hey, Cooper!" Toby could hear the pounding of

their feet closing on him.

There was a lane just ahead on the left. Wide and tree lined but with posts at the end to stop cars using it as a shortcut, it was a back way into the sports complex. If he managed to get that far he'd be able to lose Maguire, or at least be in sight of other people so, without a second thought, Toby turned down it.

Toby's feet crunched on the gravel that covered the tree lined pathway. He put on an extra burst of speed, ears peeled for the sound of pursuit. The trees shimmered and thickened and his footfalls changed from a crunch to a thud. Toby slowed to a stop and drew a few deep breaths before looking back.

There was no sign of Maguire. In fact, there was no sign of anything else familiar for that matter. He was on a stone paved road in the middle of an old forest of trees, many of a type Toby had never seen before. None of it was even vaguely recognisable. He had absolutely no idea where he was.

Chapter Eighteen

The road went straight in both directions but not knowing which one he should take he sensibly decided to sit down. This was obviously something to do with Merlin. He had started the next part of his journey; it was just in a much more dramatic fashion than he had anticipated. After sitting for a while Toby realised he was getting hungry. It appeared to be early afternoon wherever he was and Toby had no idea how long he would have to wait. In fact a small niggle of doubt now crept in. Should he wait? What if he was supposed to find his own way? But which way? Toby searched his memory for some clue as to what he should do but could find none. Convincing himself that he should wait, his next thought was to do something about the growing pangs of hunger. He rummaged through his bag and found an apple left over from his lunch. He began to munch on it enthusiastically.

The apple was almost finished when the distant clip clop of hooves made Toby look up. A group of horsemen were approaching. About twenty in number, they rode three or four abreast in no particular formation. As they neared, Toby could see swords hanging at their sides and while they appeared relaxed Toby sensed that they could have their weapons out and be ready in an instant. Toby stood as they approached. Their leader, a shorthaired warrior wearing leather armour, drew his horse to a halt and eyed Toby curiously.

"Ho there Lad. What tale brings you to be waiting in the middle of the forest?"

Before Toby could answer, a cloaked rider urged his

horse forward. "I believe he's waiting for me my lord."

"Merlin!" Toby exclaimed as the rider pulled back his hood and smiled down at him.

"Another protégé?" The leader raised an eyebrow at Merlin as Toby took the proffered hand and climbed up behind the druid.

After he settled on the rear of the saddle and the troop set off again Merlin turned his head to Toby. "You have questions?"

"Yes!" Toby was bursting with questions foremost being; "Where are we?"

"Briton"

"You mean England."

"It will be one day." Merlin replied cryptically.

Toby pondered this as he took in the forest, the road and the group of men he was now part of. "I've travelled back in time. Haven't I?"

"The year is 490AD by your modern reckoning and "travelling back" is one way of describing it. Not strictly accurate mind you but it will suffice for now."

"But..."

"Sit and enjoy the ride young Toby," Merlin said with a smile, "I promise I'll tell you all I can when we arrive."

They rode through the forest for another hour or so before the trees started thinning. Finally, they emerged from the trees into open grassland dotted with farms. Dominating the plain was a large mounded hill. The top of which was completely fortified with wooden parapets encircling it.

"Cadbury Tor," Merlin said by way of explanation as he noticed Toby's interest.

"Never heard of it," Toby commented.

"Camelot I think you call it," Merlin said, his eyes twinkling.

Toby thought about this. "Does this mean he's..." pointing at the leader

"Your Great, Great, Great... your Ancestor." Merlin

nodded. "Known as Riothalmus to some," Toby frowned. "Latin for great leader," Merlin explained, "but as you have guessed, his given name, in English, is Arthur."

Toby digested this information for a moment before asking impatiently "So, are you going to tell me what's going on now?"

Merlin laughed. "You are here to learn."

"Learn what?"

"Many things young Toby. Many things."

Merlin wouldn't elaborate no matter how much Toby pleaded but did agree to identify Arthur's other companions as they road towards the Tor. Riding next to Arthur was Caedmon, his master at arms and at his other side was Bors, Arthur's cousin. Just behind was Cador of Cornwall, Bhadvere and Hector, another relative. Merlin and Toby rode just behind them accompanied by Edwin, a young squire. Next to him rode a dark surly looking warrior, Lothar, also related to Arthur but distantly.

The rest of the troop consisted of a variety of armed men of no particular rank save that they had proven worthy enough to ride with Arthur.

They rode past the many small farms and cottages as they made their way to the base of the Tor. Toby observed the way the people were living and working with complete fascination. Everyone they passed gave some sort of friendly acknowledgement to the troop. The only thing that made Toby edgy was the intense scrutiny from Lothar. Every time he turned toward him, Lothar stared straight back, his eyes narrowed as though trying to see inside Toby. It made him feel very uneasy.

◇◇◇◇◇◇

Soon they were riding up the winding path that led to the large wooden gateway in the fortifications.

There were quite a few men peering over the top of the ramparts on either side of the gateway. As they approached, one of them waved and signalled down below. The gates swung open revealing a crowd gathered just inside. Cheering greeted them as they rode through the crowd. Many reached up to lay a hand on Arthur as he rode past and Arthur would respond with a wave, a kind word. In one instance he picked up a small curly haired girl and let her ride with him for a few paces before putting the excited child back down and leaving her with a kiss on the forehead. They halted at a long open structure, which Toby soon discovered were the stables, where they all dismounted. Merlin eased Toby to the ground before dismounting himself.

Some of the crowd diverted their attention to Toby and several people began touching his clothing and commenting how unusual it all was. Merlin noticed the attention and hurriedly moved Toby through the crowd.

"This way," Merlin said. "We need to get you looking less conspicuous." The gathering crowd parted in front of Merlin as he ushered Toby through. Merlin muttered something under his breath and the crowd seemed to lose all interest in them.

They made their way through the narrow laneways between the wooden huts until they reached a larger building.

Merlin knocked at the door. "Mistress Lilith?" he enquired.

A portly woman with a warm ruddy face appeared at the doorway. She frowned when she saw Merlin. "I have someone here who needs your ministrations," he said by way of explanation.

Mistress Lilith folded her arms, cocked an eyebrow and cast a critical eye over Toby. "Well Druid?"

"This boy here needs to be clothed"

"Aye that's obvious." There was a definite twinkle in Lilith's eye as she bantered with Merlin.

"I'd like you to find something suitable."

"Suitable eh?" Merlin nodded in agreement. "Suitable for what?" Lilith questioned.

"What?" Merlin was getting a little flustered and Toby found himself thoroughly entertained by the normally unflappable druid's discomfort.

"What does he have to be suitable for?" Lilith asked, barely holding back a smile herself.

"Well um..."

Lilith finally took pity on Merlin. "Is he going to be working in the stables?"

"Oh no I'll be presenting him to Arthur."

"Right then..." Lilith looked expectantly at Toby.

"Toby." he supplied.

"Right then young Toby, come with me," she said to Toby before calling to two other women, "Gwyneth, Alice, your help please?"

She whisked him into another room where, with a great deal of fuss (mainly from Toby), they removed his clothes tutting over each item before discarding it onto a pile in the corner, leaving Toby stark naked and doing his best to cover himself in front of these strange women.

"He's been well fed," said Gwyneth as she prodded his stomach.

"And not worked too hard," added Alice pinching his bicep.

"Leave the boy alone," said Lilith firmly. "Now let's get him dressed."

With that, she opened a wooden chest and brought out various garments which she tutted over before either putting them to one side or returning them to the chest.

Soon she appeared satisfied and closed the chest. "Now put these on," she said as she thrust the pile of clothes she selected at him.

Toby looked at the items in his arms and then looked helplessly at Lilith.

With a sigh, she took the bundle back and proceeded

to dress him.

Soon, he was standing rather self-consciously in a rough tunic and kilt. Toby shook himself trying to settle into the strange clothing.

"Can I at least keep my T-shirt?" Toby asked as he scratched himself to relieve the itching of the coarse fabric. At their blank stares, Toby indicated the shirt that was on the top of the pile of his old clothes.

Lilith rubbed the T-shirt material assessing it. "Very soft and no doubt comfortable but wouldn't last a candle mark." She tossed it aside, oblivious to Toby's pained look.

Next was footwear. Ignoring his pleas to keep his shoes they found a pair of sandals, which, with a little modification, fitted perfectly.

Soon he was back in the front room where Merlin waited to inspect him. "Most suitable Mistress Lilith," he said as he cast a critical eye over Toby's attire, "And his old garments?"

"I was going to throw them out," Lilith replied.

Merlin shook his head. "I'll take care of them if you please."

Toby breathed an inward sigh of relief. Maybe he could sneak his T-shirt underneath his tunic later.

Lilith shrugged and went back into the other room returning shortly with Toby's clothes all bundled up.

"Thank you," said Merlin as she handed them to him. "Once more you have excelled yourself."

"Why thank you druid." She replied with a big, warm smile, "I've always had a sweet spot for you too." Merlin blushed.

"That's not what I meant... I mean... I..." Toby giggled, attracting a glare from Merlin as he tried to compose himself.

"Hmmm. Yes. Well we must go. Thank you again" Merlin quickly ushered Toby out.

Chapter Nineteen

Arthur and his companions gathered outside the Great Hall, an imposing structure made of heavy timber with a large thatched roof. They were each holding a large tankard of ale, which they were using to wash the dust of the trip from their throats.

"Ah Merlin," Arthur said, acknowledging their arrival, "Come to offer an explanation as to how we happened to find this lad in the middle of the forest?"

"Chance'd be a fine thing." muttered Lothar.

Merlin ignored him and ushered Toby forward.

"I present to you Toby," he began. "A lad of distinguished lineage from distant parts and here to learn the way of a warrior."

So that was it, Toby thought.

"Come here boy," Arthur beckoned him over. "Let me look at you." He studied Toby intently for some time. "There's something familiar about you now that I see you out of that strange attire."

"Looks like you did twenty years ago," put in Bors to laughs of agreement from the rest.

"What chance Merlin?" Arthur laughed along. "Is he a relative?"

"Yes my lord, but very distant."

Arthur clapped hands on Toby's shoulder.

"Then my boy you shall have duty at my table tonight."

With that, he downed the remainder of his ale and went into the hall followed by the others.

Lothar gave Toby a departing scowl.

"I don't think he likes me," observed Toby.

"He sees you as a threat." Merlin explained.

"Why?" Toby asked but then the answer became clear.

A woman came out from the hall and wrapped a possessive arm about Lothar's waist. Recognition sent a cold chill down Toby's spine. It was 'Aunt' Fay or Morgiana as he now knew her be, younger, certainly but definitely her.

"It's her, it's Morgiana, she's here" Toby exclaimed. "What's she doing here?" Toby's level of anxiety was increasing every second. "She... she..."

"Calm young Toby, calm," Merlin said soothingly, "She's Arthur's half sister remember and is supposed to be here."

"But she knows who I am she'll..."

"Calm yourself," Merlin said. "At this point in time she has no idea who you are. For the moment she's plotting to be queen and to be that, Lothar needs to be king."

Toby became alarmed again on hearing this. "But how can Lothar be king?" Toby asked, "I thought I was Arthur's descendant"

"You are, you are," Merlin explained. "But at this time Arthur has not yet met Guinevere and even when he does," Merlin mumbled, almost to himself, "things will still not be clear."

Merlin placed a hand on Toby's shoulder and guided him away from the front of the hall. "Lothar is a powerful chieftain. If something were to happen to Arthur now, Lothar would be his most likely replacement."

Toby thought he was beginning to understand. "So she is trying to manipulate things to make that happen."

"Exactly!" Merlin exclaimed, pleased with Toby's insight.

"But she's not going to succeed is she?"

Merlin didn't reply, he merely smiled cryptically and gave Toby a conspiratal wink.

"She's like you isn't she?" Toby asked. "That's how she can be here ...er ... at home... you know what I mean!"

Merlin smiled, "Yes young Toby, I do. Morgiana has power but it comes from a dark place."

Toby frowned. Merlin sat down on a pile of logs and beckoned for Toby to sit next to him.

"There are those that are born with a gift," he explained. "We can tap into the very essence of the earth itself. Some of us choose to use this ability to help mankind, steering them on a path of peace, prosperity and being as one with the earth that supports them. But others believe the gift gives them the right to rule all others and that the earth is there to be plundered as they see fit."

"And that's who I'm fighting?" Toby asked.

"That is who we are all fighting," Merlin replied and stared out at nothing for a moment before breaking himself out of his reverie. "We must get you ready."

"For what?" Toby asked before recalling that he was supposed to do something that night at a banquet. "What does it mean to "have duty" anyway?"

"Why, you are to serve at Arthur's table tonight." Merlin replied. "It is a great honour."

"To be a waiter?" Toby was appalled.

"The best way for the young to learn the way of the world is to listen to their elders as they converse. It only makes sense that they be useful at the same time," Merlin explained. "Tonight you shall learn how the court here functions and tomorrow, all being well, you shall begin weapons training."

Merlin smiled with self-satisfaction then frowned.

"If this is what you planned why do you look so unhappy?"

"Because," Merlin responded, "for this you must be dressed properly

"And?"

Merlin sighed.

"It means we must make a return visit to Mistress Lilith."

◇◇◇◇◇◇◇

The great hall was well named. It was huge even by Toby's contemporary standards. The floor was dirt but hard packed by constant use to the point where it resembled concrete. A huge fire burned in the middle sending smoke spiralling up to a hole high in the thatched roof supported by huge wooden beams that were bigger than most trees Toby had seen. Surrounding the fire were tables at which Arthur and his companions sat.

Toby's job for the evening was quite simple. He had a wine jug and was to keep it full and at the ready. Should any of the guests require wine, he was to rush over and fill their cup. Apart from that, he was free to listen and learn.

He was not the only one. Bram, a surly youth about Toby's age, was in charge of the ale jug. He had spurned Toby's proffered greeting and, instead proceeded to 'accidentally' shove Toby whenever he had the chance. It came as no surprise to find out he was Lothar's son from an earlier marriage. However, it was in a boy named Caleb that Toby found an ally. He was Caedmon's son and even though he was a few years younger than Toby, he was open and friendly. Caleb was a font of knowledge and by the end of that evening Toby knew a great deal more about the inner workings of the court.

As the evening wore on, weariness took hold of Toby and he found himself swaying. The straw pallet in the nearby sleeping hut, assigned to him earlier, had at first looked very uncomfortable but now he couldn't think of anywhere else he wanted to be. The flow of drink eventually slowed and glowing embers were all that was left of the fire. Arthur dismissed Toby and the others for the evening. He trudged wearily to his pallet where he collapsed into an exhausted sleep. It had been a big day.

Chapter Twenty

"Ever fought with a sword before lad?"

The sun was barely up over the horizon and yet Toby was up, dressed in a padded outfit that had been laid next to his bed and had even managed some breakfast which consisted of a gritty type of porridge but still beat camp food hands down. Now he was in the middle of the training grounds facing Master at Arms Caedmon.

"No. We don't carry swords where I'm from"

"No swords?" said Caedmon in surprise. "No swords at all?"

"Well I've seen a few sword fights." Toby replied thinking of all the movies he'd watched.

"Really?" said Caedmon, raising his eyebrows and waving at a rack of wooden swords. "Grab a training sword and we'll see if you picked up anything."

Toby hesitantly went to the rack and examined the range of wooden swords. They all looked the same. Toby made a show of studying them before selecting one at random and waving it experimentally.

Caedmon grunted in apparent approval and called to Toby's companion from the night before. "Caleb?" he called. "Come over here and match up against this newcomer."

Toby made his way to the sandy area that served as a practice area. Caleb took up a position about two metres away from him and gave him a smile. Toby smiled back and adjusted his grip on the wooden training sword. Caleb, being younger, was a good head and a half shorter than Toby. The boy nodded at him to indicate readiness and Toby adopted an 'on guard' position as he'd seen done in countless films.

Seconds later, he was flat on his back, his ribs sore and with a bang on the head that would produce a nice lump later on. He struggled to his feet, ignoring the laughter from some of the others that had stopped their practice to watch.

Caedmon slapped Toby on the back. "Never mind lad. The druid can't always pick them. Let's go and get you cleaned up a bit hey?"

"No!" Toby leaned down and picked up his sword. "I'd like to try again."

"Well you've got spirit I'll give you that much." He scratched his chin thoughtfully. "All right one more try."

Others had stopped what they were doing and there was now a small crowd gathering to watch this bit of entertainment. Several began speculating the odds and soon were placing bets with others in the crowd. Toby swivelled his shoulders. His ribs hurt but he could still move freely. Caleb squared up to him.

Toby wasn't about to adopt the same 'on guard' pose he'd used last time. It was clearly something that looked good but, as his aching head could verify, had little practical value. He instead adopted a loose balanced stance similar to what Caleb was using. He was surprised how natural it felt.

They nodded at each other and Caleb swung at him. Toby reacted. There were murmurs of surprise as Toby managed to block the attack. Caleb swung again. Another successful block. Caleb tried an overhead slash. Toby neatly sidestepped it and swung back at Caleb with his own attack. A narrow miss but it still provoked a smattering of approving cheers from the crowd. Toby grinned. He was settling in now.

They traded blows; Caleb's training matched by Toby's newfound natural ability.

Sweat was trickling down their faces and both were

starting to tire when Caedmon stepped in. "Put up your swords," Caedmon said, "I'm calling it a draw."

Money changed hands and even the losers looked happy enough as the crowd dispersed with the occasional: "well done lads."

Caleb looked at Toby with a newfound respect as they both recovered their breath.

Caedmon came over and placed an affectionate hand on Caleb's shoulder. "Off you go." Caedmon said, "Tell cook to give you a spare drumstick. You earned it" The thought of food was obviously appealing and Caleb ran off without looking back.

Caedmon turned his attention to Toby. "Never picked up a sword before?" Caedmon stroked his beard thoughtfully "I should ha' known better than to second guess that druid."

As Toby smiled at the implied praise he noticed for the first time Merlin standing in the background. Merlin gave Toby the briefest nod of approval before departing in a swirl of robes.

"Well lad," Caedmon continued, "you've got talent, no doubt of that so..."

Toby was half hoping that he could also go and have an extra breakfast but instead...

"... We should teach you some skills to go with it."

Basic sword drill kept Toby busy the rest of the morning and by lunch, he was tired and famished.

Lunch consisted of some rough bread, cold meat and some cheese washed down with ale of some kind, a far cry from what he had at home but definitely better that some of what he'd eaten at camp.

After lunch, it was cleaning the stables. It was hard work and Toby suspected he would be feeling it tomorrow. Caleb's companionship eased the tedium of the work and the afternoon was enjoyable apart from one incident.

Bram, being older, had the job of cleaning and oiling the leather harnesses. They hung on a series of pegs near the doorway but Bram would take them outside where he would work on them while chatting with some others around his age.

Caleb was busy shovelling old straw and manure into a pile while Toby was raking out fresh straw when Bram, cleaned leathers in one hand, headed for the pegs. Caleb was in his way but Bram roughly shoved him aside.

Caleb stumbled, dropping his shovel. "Hoy! Watch where you're going!"

Bram ignored him and hung up the leathers before selecting another set to clean. As he turned to go out, he aimed a kick at Caleb. Caleb dodged to one side.

"What's your problem?"

"You are," Bram spat. "You didn't try this morning. You tried to make him," indicating Toby, "look good just to suck up!"

"No I didn't," Caleb retorted.

"Then that means you must just be pathetic," sneered Bram

Bram gave him another shove, this time sending him flying backwards.

Caleb said a word that Toby had never heard before. It must have been bad because Bram became furious. He picked up the fallen shovel and swung it down at Caleb.

Toby instinctively thrust his rake out, catching the shovel. It slid down the shaft of the rake and Toby spun it, twisting the shovel out of Bram's hands and throwing him off balance.

"See! Told you I didn't," said Caleb as he got to his feet and grinned triumphantly at Bram.

Bram glowered but two of them facing him were obviously more than he liked. Bram gave a final sneer and began to make his way out. It wasn't until they turned back to work that Bram spun back around and charged at Toby, catching him in the small of the back and flinging him forward. Toby twisted, narrowly missing the worst of the muck as he fell onto the stable floor.

By the time he was back on his feet, Bram had gone. Toby brushed himself down and grinned wryly. Caleb grinned back before becoming serious. "If he didn't like you before he's going to hate you now."

Toby shrugged, he was getting used to having that effect with some people.

"C'mon," Caleb continued, "we'd best get cleaned up for tonight." Toby followed Caleb out from the stables. They were required to serve at table again that night and Toby was hoping he would have a chance to talk to Merlin alone. He had been here a full day now and hadn't spoken to him since their arrival. He rather wanted to know how long he was going to be here.

It was still dark when a splash of cold water on his face roused Toby. Bleary eyed, he followed the others to the great hall where he discovered they were also responsible for cleaning it up, something he'd been reprieved from the first night. Breakfast followed and then his training began in earnest.

The daily routine was now set. Mornings, filled with intense training from Caedmon, where his skills quickly developed so he was sparring with and regularly beating those much older and more experienced. Afternoons, the stables, though occasionally Arthur summoned him to run an errand, causing the odd jealous glance from some of the others - usually those that hung around with Bram. Each time he appeared before Arthur, Toby hoped he would see Merlin. He still hadn't spoken to him since that first day only catching an occasional glimpse of him during training.

It seemed they were required to serve table each night, though thankfully some nights things wound down earlier than others, after which, Toby would crawl onto his pallet and fall into an exhausted but happy sleep.

Several days passed and the initial aching of muscles

used as they had never been before faded. One ache wouldn't fade. They'd kept him so busy with training and other duties that he barely had time to think of home but when he did, it hurt. He missed his bed he missed his friends, he missed going for rides on his bike, he even missed school. But mostly he missed his parents. He only hoped that they weren't too worried but suspected they would be frantic. A boy going missing would have made it into the papers, possibly even the TV. Toby wished there was a way he could let them know he was safe and not to worry. It was these times, usually late at night, he felt like crying, just a little. Several times, he even got himself out of bed with the intention of finding Merlin and demanding to go home. The only thing stopping him was he didn't know where Merlin was.

Finally, one morning Merlin appeared just as they were finishing breakfast. He beckoned for Toby to follow him, causing a few curious glances between the others.

Merlin led Toby back to the great hall where they sat themselves down near the fire pit, to benefit from the lingering warmth that still radiated from it.

"So young Toby," Merlin began. "How are you faring?"

Toby considered this for a moment and tears began to well, "I miss home."

"Of course you do," Merlin said. "You wouldn't be the boy I thought you were if you didn't."

"I think I can put a bit of your mind at ease at least," he added.

"Really?" Toby asked.

"Your parents aren't worried about you."

"Oh good!" Relief was Toby's first emotion followed quickly by a bit of resentment. "Why not?"

Merlin sighed. "Time here and time at home aren't the same," he explained. "Even though months may pass here, only a second will have passed at home. That means when you go home," he placed a comforting hand on Toby's shoulder, "and I promise that will be soon, you will return only a moment after you left."

Toby felt like a weight had lifted from him. Freed of the worry about his parents he could now enjoy his training without feeling guilty.

"But that is not why I called you aside young Toby," Merlin's sombre tone snapped Toby out of his reverie, "You have made an enemy in Bram."

"Couldn't really avoid it," Toby shrugged.

"No, you couldn't," said Merlin. "And even if you'd tried you'd have been unsuccessful."

Seeing Toby's quizzical look, Merlin continued. "Bram's father is obsessed with why you are here, no doubt encouraged by Morgiana. That obsession turned to suspicion, which became dislike. Bram feels duty bound to dislike you as well, the fact he is a bully and you stood up to him has only intensified this."

Toby screwed up his eyes. "So why are you telling me this again?"

"Just letting you know you need to be extra cautious. It is not unknown for there to be deaths during training and that, my young friend, is something your parents would notice."

Merlin stood, patted Toby on the shoulder and left him to ponder that sobering thought.

Chapter Twenty-One

Toby threw himself into training and within no time, he had progressed to where he was regularly beating the older boys with whom he was sparring. On rare occasions, he sparred with Bram who was widely acknowledged as the best of the trainees. After being soundly beaten the first time they sparred Toby managed to hold his own, much to the surprise of everyone.

His rapid advance did not make him any more popular with Bram and his friends. There were several verbal threats, though none of them ever really tried anything apart from the occasional trip whenever they thought they could get away with it. Even then, the ever alert Caedmon often caught them. Sending them, as punishment to clean out the pigsty as, in his words, pigs weren't disciplined either.

Their taunts and threats reminded Toby of Maguire but there was one big difference, Maguire would not have lasted five minutes. Here, actions had consequences. Here if you pushed someone they might just push back but with a sword and there would be nobody who would step in and break it up.

On an increasing number of occasions, he caught sight of 'Aunt' Fay. She would often appear at training with Lothar. They would stand, her arm possessively entwined in his, as Lothar watched Bram. Morgiana however watched Toby. Occasionally she would whisper something into Lothar's ear and he would look at Toby and frown.

At those times, he would often catch a glimpse of

Merlin who made sure they were aware of his presence. At the sight of him, they would quickly leave, though not without giving Toby a final glare.

◇◇◇◇◇◇◇

One afternoon Merlin appeared at the stables and beckoned for Toby to follow him, stating in a voice loud enough for the others to hear that Arthur had an errand for him that would take the rest of the day. Toby obediently followed but was confused when, instead of heading toward the great hall, a place he'd found Arthur for previous errands, they headed to a quiet spot behind the kitchens.

When Merlin was sure there was no one around he faced Toby.

"Now the real reason I took you aside is I must ask you to be extra cautious for a time." Merlin said. "I must attend to some urgent matters and will be away."

"Okay." Toby replied warily.

"This means, young Toby, that I won't be able to keep an eye on you."

"So you have been watching me?" said Toby, thinking of those times during training.

"It has been necessary." Merlin explained. "Not all here are your friends as you have gathered and they might take this opportunity to act."

"Act?" Toby was now getting nervous.

"Calm." Merlin said reassuringly. "I do not expect them to try anything but I would be remiss if I did not warn you. Don't be provoked and if anything out of the ordinary happens, be extra alert."

Toby nodded in understanding but then gave Merlin an intense look. "Merlin? How much longer will I be here?"

"Getting homesick my boy?"

"A little."

"Well, your training is almost complete." Merlin clapped his hand reassuringly on Toby's shoulder. "You're doing very well."

It wasn't until Merlin had left him that Toby realised he hadn't answered his question.

That night the mood in the great hall was slightly different. Toby wasn't sure if it was Merlin's absence but Lothar seemed more outspoken and the occasional looks he gave Toby were smug, even contemptuous rather than the normal brooding glares.

Toby stayed closer to the tables that night than usual. He was hoping to find out what Merlin was up to. There was a lot of speculation, including one rumour that Merlin was turning himself into a dragon to scare the Saxons, but no one seemed to know anything definite and Arthur, when quizzed, seemed unusually evasive.

At one point Caedmon attracted his attention and indicated his goblet was in need of a refill

As Toby made his way towards him Lothar stuck his foot out, catching Toby's ankle. He stumbled and sprawled on the floor spilling his jug all over himself in the process.

"Clumsy lout," Lothar declared. "Bram, see to Caedmon's wine," he continued, indicating a jug in front of him. "A man would die of thirst with this one around." There was some laughter at Toby's expense as Bram grabbed the indicated jug and filled Caedmon's cup.

Toby stood back up and tried to clean himself up but the mixture of wine with the earthen floor meant there was no hope of that. Arthur looked him over and excused him for the rest of the evening.

After cleaning himself up, Toby went to his bed but couldn't sleep. Merlin's warning coupled with tonight's incident had his mind in such a whirl that he couldn't relax. He was still awake as the others returned. Some pretended to trip over things while others made what they thought were witty comments like 'can't hold his drink' or 'I thought the druid was the one taking a trip'. Eventually they all settled and left Toby alone with his thoughts. It was very late when Toby finally managed to drift off.

◇◇◇◇◇◇◇

The next morning there was no sign of Caedmon. Toby waited with the others in the practice ground with an increasing degree of apprehension. Something just didn't feel right. Caedmon had never missed a lesson before now and there seemed to be a lot of spectators gathering which was something Caedmon usually discouraged. Toby's thoughts went back to his last talk with Merlin. Anything unusual he'd said. Toby was beginning to think that this qualified.

His fears were confirmed when Lothar strode onto the training ground.

"I'll be taking over training this morning," he announced. "Seems Caedmon is unwell, something he had last night no doubt." Bram snickered at this.

Toby recalled last night's incident. This was planned.

"Time to see what you're made of boy." Lothar tossed a sword to him. "No toy blades in my lessons. Bram?" He called his son over. Bram was obviously prepared for this as he already had his sword out.

Bram was a good head taller than he was and a lot broader. Bram made a couple of swings then settled into a fighting stance grinning at him.

Toby hefted his sword. The balance felt wrong. He'd handled several other real swords in the last couple of weeks and knew enough to realise this was not a good sword. A knot formed in Toby's stomach as he realised that this wasn't supposed to be a fair fight.

"On yer guard." Lothar yelled. Toby barely got into his fighting stance before Bram made his first swing. Toby blocked it but awkwardly. The unbalanced sword threw him off. Bram attacked again and once more Toby only just managed to deflect it. He ran back several paces, provoking a few rude shouts from the crowd, but he was just getting enough distance so he could settle and adjust his technique. Bram came at him again and this time Toby deflected it easily. He then side stepped and swung a blow at Bram. He parried but not convincingly. In fact Bram seemed surprised and looked in confusion toward Lothar. It was obvious that he was surprised Toby was fighting back so well and things were not quite going to plan.

Toby took the initiative and sent a series of awkward attacks at Bram who only just managed to block them. Bram was obviously rattled. He may have had the physical advantage but now Toby had a psychological edge.

Bram tried several more attacks but each time Toby managed to parry, Bram lost a little bit more confidence.

Toby's sword arm was beginning to hurt. Wielding the unbalanced blade was putting a lot of strain on it. He needed to finish this somehow before his arm gave way. He hadn't beaten Bram in their occasional sparring but had noticed Bram tended to leave his left side exposed. Toby feinted to his left, causing Bram to lash out defensively but Toby had already spun around to his right. Bram was left exposed and off balance. Toby swung at him as hard as he could. At the last minute, he shifted his grip and twisted the sword's blade so that the flat of it whacked Bram solidly on the backside, sending him sprawling in the dirt. Laughter burst out of the crowd accompanied by some enthusiastic applause. Bram scrambled back to his feet his face bright with embarrassment. Toby stood there watching him, sword in hand and smiling. He took one look at Toby, turned and fled.

Toby made his way off the training field but Lothar stopped him.

"Where do you think you're going?" Lothar roared at him. "I haven't finished with you."

Toby's heart fell as Lothar strode out to the field and brandished his sword.

"Let's see what you've got," Lothar said as he immediately launched an attack at Toby

Toby parried but the jolt it sent down his arm almost numbed it. Lothar was strong. Toby managed to deflect the next attack and the next but then Lothar, using his strength, swiped at Toby's sword

The sheer power of the swing ripped the unbalanced sword out of Toby's grip and sent it spinning through the air to land across the far side of the field. Toby was standing unarmed and helpless.

There was some polite applause from the crowd that had gathered around but most had realised it was an unfair contest

There being no point in bitterness, Toby forced a smile at Lothar, and bowed acknowledging his victory. Lothar smiled back then swung at him again. Only Toby's reflexes allowed him to jump out of the way in time.

"Did ya think the fight was over when you lost your sword?" Lothar laughed and swung again. Once more Toby was lucky to dodge the blow. "Now for your lesson," Lothar said.

"What am I suppose to learn from this?" Toby asked.

Lothar leaned down to his ear and whispered, "How to die."

Toby gulped at the malicious smile Lothar gave him.

Another swing and another near miss.

Toby stumbled, fell but scrambled to his knees in time to see Lothar preparing an overhead blow that Toby had no doubt would slice him right down the middle.

"No!" The cry came from the depth of his being. He was not prepared to die. He flung his hand up defensively as warmth radiated through his body and as he did so felt the hilt of Excalibur against his palm. Instinctively he gripped it and turned his defence into an aggressive upswing that met Lothar's blade and shattered it.

The crowd went silent. Several crossed themselves while others made signs to ward off evil.

Lothar stared stunned at the remains of his sword then, slowly, his gaze shifted to Toby. Toby stared back coldly and Lothar's eyes widened in fright. He dropped what was left of his sword and took several paces back.

"Witchery!" Lothar's finger pointed accusingly straight at Toby. "This boy is Satan's spawn. Take him."

Several of the crowd drew swords and made their way toward him.

Toby adopted a fighting stance and waited. They were wary and spread out so some of them would be able to outflank him. He was going to lose he realised. He might be able to take one or two with him but to what purpose. It would only convince everyone that Lothar was right. If he gave up, he may have a slight chance particularly if Merlin explained things.

He stood straight and put up his sword releasing his grip on it. The sword vanished causing another collective gasp of astonishment and temporarily stopping the men advancing toward him.

In fact, doubts were creeping into several of their minds. He was, after all, related to Arthur. Merlin vouched for him and everyone knew the druid was on their side. Moreover, it wasn't a fair fight so who could blame the boy if he used a trick to save his life.

Lothar could see the tide turning. "No!" he cried. "He is evil and must be destroyed." Lothar tried to rally the mob but the sound of galloping hooves made them turn. Merlin on a horse, his robes billowing out behind him, bore down on them. They scattered before him

"Grab my arm boy," Merlin called as he rapidly approached.

Merlin scooped down as Toby leapt for his arm.

Merlin grabbed him and swung him up onto the saddle behind him. They galloped off across the field, narrowly avoiding a final desperate grab from Lothar, and sped through the village.

Within minutes, they were out of the compound and galloping down the hill back toward the forest. Only when they reached the safety of the trees did Merlin ease back on the horse.

Chapter Twenty-Two

"Well that was a near thing," Merlin observed as they trotted along the road that led through the forest. Toby could only nod in agreement. Merlin steered the horse off the road and down a narrow path that led to a stream. He let Toby down and grabbed a bag that was hanging off the saddle.

"Your clothes," Merlin said by way of explanation. "I got them from Mistress Lilith just after you arrived. You'll also find some soap in there. Wash yourself in the stream."

Toby just stood there. "Wash?" he said in confusion.

"You smell like the stables and I'm sure you don't want to go home smelling like that."

"Home?" Toby asked in disbelief.

"Home," replied Merlin.

In no time, Toby had stripped and was lathering himself up in the creek.

"So I'm finished with training?" he asked as he soaped up his hair a second time.

"You have achieved all that you needed to here," was Merlin's reply, cryptic as usual.

Toby cocked an eyebrow at him and reached down to the creek bed where he found a large handful of mud.

"Just what did I achieve here then?" Toby asked while casually holding the mud in a throwing manner.

"Humpphh!" Merlin's eyebrows went up and down a couple of times. "Well... Hmmpphhh."

Toby just looked at him expectantly while moving

the handful of mud much in the same way as a shot putter does just before they throw.

"Well if you must know," Merlin said. "There were two things. One was to learn not only how to use a sword but to call Excalibur when you need it. That is what you achieved this morning."

"Risky way to learn it," Toby said, thinking back to the fight with Lothar.

"Yes, but a risk worth taking as it turns out."

"And the other thing?" he asked, not quite ready to relinquish his mud.

"Ah," said Merlin, "that was a little more complicated. I needed to thwart Morgiana's plans at this time."

Toby frowned. "How did I do that?" he asked as he let the mud wash away.

"She was going to use Lothar and gather enough support behind him to take over from Arthur. Now that you have shown him up, he will never be able to get that support." Merlin looked extraordinarily pleased with himself. "Well done," he added.

"But what about the witch thing and being spawn of something?"

Merlin was dismissive. "Some will believe it, but most will see it as Lothar attempting to blame something else for his weakness."

"And the fact that Excalibur popped out of thin air?"

"They will pretend not to have seen it, much in the same way no one at home will notice that your hair is longer and more untidy."

Toby looked at his reflection in the water and grimaced.

"Speaking of which it's time to get you going." He threw Toby a large cloth to dry himself with.

Toby stared at Merlin who, after a moment of realisation, turned his back so Toby could get out of the creek, dry himself and get dressed in his old clothes.

Merlin cast a critical eye over him. "Yes, apart from the hair and a few extra muscles you look as you did when you arrived. Ready?"

Toby nodded.

"Good. Now close your eyes."

There was a slight lurch.

"Merlin, can I open my eyes yet?" Toby asked.

There was no answer. "Merlin?" Still nothing. He cautiously opened his eyes and looked around. He was back. Standing right in the middle of the laneway that he'd left what seemed like ages ago. He breathed a huge sigh of relief. Then he heard it. Shouts of "There he is!" and with a start, Toby realised that Maguire was still chasing him. He'd come back to the exact minute he'd left.

Toby almost used the word that he'd heard his father use last time he hit his thumb with a hammer but refrained, instead he ran, mentally cursing Merlin for not at least putting him back a bit further away.

Down the lane he pelted. He was running faster than he'd ever run. One thing was for sure, the months of living and training in dark ages Briton had left Toby a lot fitter than he'd ever been. There was a sports ground a bit further along. If he was lucky, he might be able lose them there. He turned the corner and ... WHAM!

Toby fell in a tangle of arms and legs. Picking himself up, he saw who he'd barrelled into.

"Peter, what are you doing here?"

"It was a short practice," Peter replied, as he got back to his feet. "What's the hurry?"

"Maguire and friends."

Peter did use the word and picked up his equipment that had been scattered by their impact. Toby quickly helped all the while looking for the best way to go. The tennis courts were back in the direction Peter had come but they were too far. There was a bunch of people standing strangely under a tree straight ahead and in the other direction some juniors practising football. Toby decided the people under the tree was the best option but was too late.

"Well, well, well, Cooper and the tennis wuss!" Maguire and his cronies had arrived. "This will be fun."

Toby noticed that each of them was carrying thick sticks that they were brandishing about like makeshift clubs. Peter used the word again.

They were both in trouble and Toby didn't feel like running anymore. He briefly considered trying to call Excalibur forth but decided that would be overkill (besides he'd only done it once so it might not work).

Instead, he reached down, grabbed one of Peter's tennis racquets and adopted a fighting stance. Maguire grinned maliciously at Toby as he made a mocking impersonation of Toby's stance. Toby wasn't sure if it meant that Maguire was confident or just too stupid to realise what the stance meant. Toby suspected the latter.

Billy and Warren spread out, getting themselves in to a position to attack from the side, all the while waving their clubs menacingly.

Peter started backing away and Billy went for him. Toby stepped across and blocked the club as it came whistling down, stopping it inches from a stunned Peter's head. He reversed and brought the racquet down on Billy's wrist. Billy screamed in pain and dropped his club. Maguire came for him and Toby ducked under the blow with a roll. Coming back to his feet, he prepared himself to launch a counter attack but he couldn't. Maguire was gone. Toby went and looked back down the lane. Maguire, Warren and Billy, now nursing his wrist, were running down it as fast as they could.

A hand fell on Toby's shoulder.

"Gotcha!" Toby tried to shrug the hand off but it was gripping too tight. He twisted around to face this new opponent. It was an adult. By the tracksuit and whistle, Toby could only assume it was one of the football coaches.

"It ..." Toby began to explain.

"Save it," the coach responded, "until your parents come down. Then you can explain what you were doing."

Chapter Twenty-Three

The coach marched them to the football clubhouse without saying a word. Even when he'd dragged them inside the only time he spoke to them was to ask their name and phone number. He left them sitting on a rickety bench in the change room while he went into the office, a small glass and wood cubicle taking up one corner, where he picked up the phone and dialled.

"Hello Mrs Hays?" the Coach said to the phone. Mrs Hays? Toby thought, that was Billy's Mum.

Toby and Peter strained to hear more but the coach lowered his voice. He spoke to Billy's mother for about five minutes. After hanging up he stood and stared at them through the glass, arms folded as if trying to think of what to do next. He picked up the phone again and dialled.

"Hello Frank, it's Sam from the footy club here. I have a couple of your students here."

Frank? Who from the school was called Frank? Then it clicked and any hope of fairness fled as they realised that this second call was to Mr Lloyd. They must know each other

"Toby Cooper and Peter DeSilva," he said in obvious answer to a question from Mr Lloyd. "Yes Cooper, Toby Cooper…. Well it seems they ganged up on Billy Hays…. No he wasn't alone; Stanley and Warren came and helped him when they saw what was happening."

Toby and Peter stared at each other open mouthed. This version of events was so far away from the truth as to be a joke. The coach became aware of their interest and turned his back, once again lowering his voice.

The call to Mr Lloyd finally ended and Toby took the opportunity to knock on the office door.

"Sir," he began, "if I could just explain..."

"I'm not interested," the coach cut him off. "Mr Lloyd warned me about you two and I don't want to hear whatever story you have concocted while sitting there. The school is going to sort everything out Monday and now that I have all the facts, I'm going to call your parents."

◇◇◇◇◇◇

Tense silence dominated the drive home. His mother's tight lips and the fact that she wouldn't look at him were indication that he was in a lot of trouble. The coach had made sure that they couldn't overhear as he detailed the incident to his and Peter's mother but his mother's reaction since then told him it wasn't good.

His father was already home by the time they arrived and Toby expected the questions to begin, but instead they told him to wait in his room until dinner was ready.

As he waited, sitting idly on his bed, he realised it had been months since he'd seen it. He sniffed. There was a slightly bad smell that he hadn't noticed until now. He sniffed again. Yep, definitely bad! He looked under his bed thinking that he may have left school lunch under there accidentally but there was nothing there except a box of old toys and a couple of socks which, after careful sniffing, surprisingly weren't the source of the smell. After searching the room he made the startling discovery that the smell was coming from him. Obviously the scrub in the creek hadn't been quite thorough enough and a shower was definitely in order.

Hot water and soap! It's amazing how good it can make you feel. Toby stepped out of the shower clean, refreshed and feeling thoroughly back home. He eyed himself critically in the mirror. His hair was definitely longer than it should be and very ragged, the result no doubt of trimming it with a knife – there being no barbers in dark ages Briton. Still, if he brushed it back Merlin might be right and no one would notice.

As he went back to his room he could hear the faint murmur of his parents talking in the kitchen but wasn't game to sneak down and listen at the door. He figured he was in enough trouble without being caught eavesdropping.

Barely a word was spoken over dinner and it wasn't until they'd finished and Toby had, without being asked and hoping to gain a bit of favour, washed and dried the dishes that the questioning started.

His parents sat opposite him at the table and it was his mother who began.

"Well Toby, would you care to offer an explanation for this afternoon?"

At last, a chance to tell his side of the story. Toby launched into a detailed account of his trip home from school, the chase and finally, the encounter at the sports field. He carefully omitted any reference to travelling back in time and meeting King Arthur as he felt his credibility was on thin enough ice already.

"Why were they chasing you?" his father asked as he finished.

"Well…" It was at that point he realised he had no reasonable answer. The whole series of incidents and encounters that had built up over time and escalated since the school camp were something that Toby had kept from his parents. "He just doesn't like me." Toby finished lamely.

His parents exchanged a meaningful look.

"Toby," his mother began, "I'm afraid the other boys are telling a completely different story."

"Then ask Peter if you don't believe me?" he blurted in desperation.

"We'd like to believe you but …." His mother looked helplessly at him and his father took over.

"Billy's parents rang and they think his arm might be broken. They are considering legal action but we've all spoken to the school and we have agreed to let the school sort things out on Monday. All we can do is hope you won't be expelled."

Some hope. They didn't know Maguire and had no idea of his favoured status at school.

"In the meantime we need to decide what to do with you."

His punishment, they decided, was simple. They grounded him. No weekend bike rides, no detours to the shops on the way home and definitely no hanging around with Peter. He would be dropped off at school in the morning and picked up after it and, for good measure, no television.

That got to him. No television. It shouldn't have worried him. After all he'd spent the last few months without missing it at all but now, knowing that it was just in the next room and that his favourite show was on tonight (there are some things you don't forget even after spending months in the dark ages) having it taken away made him realise just how upset his parents were with him.

Downcast, he mumbled an apology and trudged his way upstairs.

◇◇◇◇◇◇◇

He woke early the next morning. It was light but the sun was yet to put in an appearance. Newly acquired habits made Toby almost leap out of bed but then he remembered. No hall to tidy, no stables to clean and no sword practice. He snuggled back down enjoying the luxury of his soft warm bed and tried to go back to sleep but he was now so used to early starts he became restless. It was as though he was too comfortable. Annoyed with himself, he sat up and looked at the clock. It was just on six o'clock. If he got up now what could he do? He couldn't go out anywhere – he was grounded, he couldn't go down for breakfast - not without raising all sorts of awkward questions, the most searching of which would be 'why was he up?' as he normally didn't put in an appearance much before eight-thirty on a weekend. There was probably some homework he should be doing but he couldn't remember what it was supposed to be, even if he had wanted to.

He lay back down and ran events of the past few months through his mind. He didn't want to forget anything. He especially wanted to keep the sword fighting techniques he'd learned fresh in his mind. The thought made him smile. Caedmon had often said that a good swordsman used his mind. Now, without a sword, it was all Toby could use... unless... of course...

Excalibur!

He had a sword. His sword.

Toby leapt out of bed, excited that he'd found something to do.

He quickly dressed; rationalising that sword practice shouldn't be done in pyjamas, and stood there poised and ready.

Now all he needed to do was figure out how he'd got Excalibur into his hand last time.

He remembered back to what he'd done in his fight with Lothar, going through each move until Excalibur had magically appeared and turned the tide of battle.

He'd been on his knees, arm raised defensively and Excalibur had appeared. He adopted the pose as he remembered it.

Nothing!

He tried the pose again.

Still nothing!

Maybe if he shifted his arm slightly... He caught sight of himself in the full length mirror on the back of his door. He looked ridiculous. This was obviously not the way to get Excalibur off the chain around his neck and into his hand.

He sat on his bed and ran the fight through his mind again. It made him shiver to realise how close he'd come to death and... perhaps emotion was the key? He tried to remember how he was feeling during the fight. Fear – there'd been a lot of that all the way through the fight. Anger – yes he'd been angry, but there were times recently when he'd been angrier so that probably wasn't it. What had he been feeling at that moment? Take away the fear and anger, what had he been thinking as Lothar swung his sword down toward his head. He wanted to live... was determined to live because there was so much left to do.

That was it; determination.

He stood back up and thought about how much he wanted Excalibur.

Nothing!

Not to be discouraged he tried again, this time clearing his mind and then focusing it on Excalibur, willing it to be in his hand.

Nothing!

Toby frowned. No, not quite nothing. He was sure he detected a slight warming where Excalibur dangled against his chest.

Encouraged, he tried again. Yes! Definitely a warmth coming from the sword.

He took a deep breath and focused, willing Excalibur with every bit of determination he could gather. Sweat beaded on his forehead from concentration but it seemed to be working.

The warmth increased until it almost became unbearably hot then suddenly the heat streaked from his chest, up his arm to his hand which he now closed around the hilt of Excalibur.

He had done it!

He was so pleased with himself he almost didn't hear the slight popping sound behind him.

He turned just in time to see a small scroll drop to the carpet.

Toby released Excalibur, which promptly vanished, returning to its usual spot around his neck, and reached down for the scroll. He broke the wax seal and unrolled it.

Well done young Toby. Now that you have found the way, it will be easier and with practice will become second nature.

You have more challenges to face but remember you are not alone. Others will be there to help. Often when you least expect it.

Your journey is continuing

It wasn't signed but it had to be from Merlin. Toby was pleased that he was keeping an eye on him and then, quite alarmed by the idea. He was in his bedroom and Merlin was watching everything! Then he thought about it. There were other times when Merlin hadn't seemed to know what was going on so he couldn't always be watching. Rather, Toby expected, this was just part of the concealment spell, designed to pop out the first time he figured out how to get Excalibur by himself without the heat of battle. Toby breathed a sigh of relief. Merlin watching him all the time didn't bear thinking about particularly when it came to the bathroom!

That sorted, he tried again and Merlin's note was right. It was easier. Each time he found himself having to concentrate less to make Excalibur appear while sending it back was as simple as letting go. Toby spent the next couple of hours bringing it out and sending it back and by the time he went down for breakfast he could summon it by merely stretching his hand upward and mentally saying 'Excalibur'.

◇◇◇◇◇◇

Breakfast was a disaster. His mother made a hot breakfast, which was something of a rarity. Sausages, eggs, bacon and grilled tomato served with thick toast covered in butter. His mother put his plate down in front of him and Toby, without thinking, picked a sausage up with his hand and began to eat.

"Toby!" his mother exclaimed in horror.

"What?" he said innocently as he absentmindedly waved the half eaten sausage around. He followed his mother's gaze and realised. "Oh, sorry." Months without cutlery had made him forget the niceties of eating.

He put the sausage down on his plate, wiped his hand on a napkin and picked up his knife and fork.

His mother eyed him critically. She reached over and ran a hand through his hair. At first Toby thought she was comforting him but then he realised she was inspecting it.

"Right," she said as she finished. "It's a trip to the barbers for you this morning. I don't know how I could have let you leave the house looking like that." Shaking her head she turned her attention to her own breakfast leaving Toby to finish his but he'd lost his appetite. He hated the barbers. His regular one was old and always wore too much aftershave - possibly in attempt to cover the reek of stale cigarette smoke. He also didn't believe in deodorant and every time he lifted his arm to take another snip Toby almost passed out. Toby until now had been content to go back up to his room and practice with Excalibur some more but now it would have to wait.

151

Chapter Twenty-Four

Toby scratched his head. He always felt itchy after going to the barbers. At least they'd been early and Antonio or Tony as he preferred to be called hadn't had a chance to smoke much or work up a sweat.

He stood facing himself in the mirror. Even he had to admit the haircut was an improvement. He held his hand up giving the briefest flicker of concentration and Excalibur appeared. He gave it a couple of experimental swings, smiling as it wove patterns in the air and set down to practice.

Its perfect balance made it far easier to use than any of the practice equipment. This ease of use was compensated somewhat by his jeans. Modern clothing just didn't appear to be designed for sword fighting. He almost wished he could have brought some of his dark ages clothing back with him. Then he remembered the constant itchiness and the fact that he would look ridiculous walking down the street dressed like that and decided he would just have to get used to using a sword in his normal clothing.

He adopted a fighting stance and went through a few set moves to warm himself up. He then ran through some of the more advanced sequences he'd learned, all the time watching himself in the mirror. He realised his fighting style was very much like Arthur's. Caedmon often had them watch the other warriors fight, getting them to imagine themselves following their moves. Toby suspected Caedmon would have loved a couple of full length mirrors.

Toby decided to go through some scenarios. He

imagined he was being attacked by two people then four then two more but this time armed with quarter staffs. He joined the moves he knew together to create a seamless flow with Excalibur weaving a complex pattern in the air as it darted to and fro depending on the imagined situation. After a couple of hours of this he finally slowed down, releasing Excalibur and sitting on his bed to catch his breath.

He was exhilarated and apart from where an over enthusiastic thrust had sent Excalibur's blade through his wardrobe door and a backhand swing had wiped out his bedside lamp, he hadn't caused any problems.

He covered the hole in his wardrobe door by sticking a poster over it. As for the lamp, it was pale blue with a base shaped like a teddy bear with more teddy bears printed on its shade or at least that's what it would look like if it wasn't in several pieces. Toby hated it and had tried several times to get rid of it but, unfortunately it had been a gift from Toby's well meaning grandmother when he was three and his mother wouldn't let him change it. In fact his grandma still asked about it every time he saw her. He examined the pieces. There was no way to fix it (not that he wanted to) and he was going to get in trouble for breaking it. At least, he rationalised, if he got in more trouble now, he'd hardly notice any extra punishment.

The practice had taken his mind off everything, but now it all came flooding back. He flopped back on his bed; the high of his practice now replaced by the low that thinking of the injustice he was suffering had brought on. He wondered how Peter was getting on. He hadn't been able to ring him (use of the phone was also banned) so he had no idea how his parents had reacted. Peter was only involved because he was a friend. Maguire had no real interest in him. He could have run away from Maguire and co. yesterday and they wouldn't have bothered him. But he hadn't, he'd stayed and confronted Maguire. It was an act of sheer bravery and it had got him in trouble. Toby sat up. Instead of lying about, feeling sorry for himself, he needed a plan, a way to get the truth out and, if nothing else, get Peter out of trouble.

Monday was the key, Toby thought. Something this serious would require the attention of the principal and therein lay his best chance. The principal would want to hear from both sides and if Toby presented his case properly he may just get a fair hearing. The problem was the only time he had spoken to the principal was to deliver a message. He'd been so nervous that he'd forgotten what he was supposed to say and began to stutter.

There had to be a way to make himself less nervous. Perhaps if he wrote down what he wanted to say he could memorise it like a script. It had to be worth a try.

Toby spent the rest of the day writing down his account of yesterday afternoon. He laid down all the facts (well not quite all) then rehearsed his statement until he knew it backwards.

It was getting dark as he finished and he was soon called down for dinner. Pizza, which meant he didn't have to worry about not using his hands at least.

He was told firmly that there would be no television for him tonight either and he might as well go to bed. Toby was surprised to find himself very tired and he didn't argue. His first full day back in his own time had been an interesting one.

◇◇◇◇◇◇◇

Sunday morning breakfast was once again hot but this time Toby refrained from eating with his hands.

"I think we should go for a drive," Toby's father announced as he folded up the Sunday paper.

"But I'm grounded," Toby said. It was the first excuse that came to mind.

"Just because you're grounded doesn't mean we

can't go for a family trip," his father responded with a certain degree of grandeur.

Toby groaned inwardly while plastering what he hoped was an excited look on his face.

His mother soon shooed him upstairs to get ready while she organised herself and his father got the car packed. Trouble with these trips was often his father was the only one who knew where they were going so getting ready posed many dilemmas. Toby dressed in jeans and a t-shirt but for shoes he opted for a sturdy pair of hiking boots just to be on the safe side. Ever since he'd given his father a book on national parks, including details of local bush walks and suggested daytrips it seemed they'd been methodically working their way through the book, so hiking boots were becoming a fairly safe bet. His mother had made a similar assumption and had packed a lunch as most of the places in the book were bereft of any form of shops.

They finally set off about ten and soon were winding their way up into the hills. Every now and then they would pull over and his father would examine the book and after the fifth occasion Toby began to wish he'd just bought him a tie.

"I thought you had memorised the book," his mother observed as they pulled over once more.

"I thought I had," his father replied. "But the other night I was browsing through it again and I found a couple of pages I couldn't recall seeing before. I think they must have been stuck together."

Toby was now more alert. Pages appearing in a book smelt of magic. Of course the pages could have been stuck together but to Toby's mind it all seemed a little too suspicious. The only thing he was worried about is if it was something other than just being 'stuck' who had done it? If it was Merlin or one of the mysterious 'others' then it was probably safe but if Morgiana was involved then he could be walking into a giant trap.

"So what is this place we're looking for?" he asked hoping to find some clue.

"You'll just have to wait and see," his father replied infuriatingly.

They drove for another ten minutes and then with an "ah hah" his father turned up what looked like a fire trail. The cars tyres crunched on gravel as they drove through the thick sub tropical rainforest that formed the main part of this park. The trail was so narrow and the forest so thick that they almost needed the headlights on. After a few more minutes the trees thinned and the trail widened until they burst out into the open to find they were near the rocky crest of a mountain.

There was a gravelled area surrounded by log rails that was set aside as parking and beyond it a couple of picnic benches. Just near them was the start of a walking track that led up to the peak. His father pulled into a spot next to the car park's only other occupant, one of the mid size four wheel drives that were so popular these days.

Toby felt inexplicably excited. His birthmark began to get the first tingles of an itch and Toby took this as a definite sign that his being here was no coincidence. He leapt out, eager to follow the track up to the peak but he was thwarted. "I think we should have lunch before we do anything else," his mother announced.

His father agreed and Toby was forced to sit impatiently at one of the picnic tables as his mother laid out bread rolls, boiled eggs, ham, cheese and salad for them.

He fidgeted restlessly through the meal, itching, literally, to explore the hill. Something about the rocky peak was calling to him in the same way the lake where he'd found Excalibur had.

Finally the meal wound up and the picnic packed away.

"Let us go for a walk," his father announced. Toby

leapt to his feet so quickly that his father cocked an eyebrow in surprise. "Well, you're very keen today," he observed. "Must be being cooped up in your room eh?" Toby grinned to avoid having to answer. "Off we go then." And with that, his father headed for the steep path.

For as long as Toby could remember his father had always been excited by exploring new places. He always used to charge off leaving Toby and his mother to struggle along behind. Today however Toby was having no trouble keeping up. Months of daily sword training had improved Toby's fitness level substantially. Add to that his desire to discover what connection he had with the mountain and he found no difficulty in keeping up with his father.

His father seemed quite surprised to see Toby keeping pace but there was also a hint of pride in the look he gave Toby as they continued up toward the peak. There were several stops on the way up containing 'interpretive signage'; in other words signs that explained things. Toby's father stopped at each one and dutifully read the information before pointing out the interesting bits to Toby. From it he learned that Baxter's Peak, as it was called, was the remnant core of a long extinct volcano. It was named after an unfortunate amateur explorer who had the unhappy knack of discovering places not long after someone else had. He quickly earned the distinction (if you could call it that) of being the second person to visit more places than any one else. He despaired of this and one day set off into the rainforest never to be seen again. His body was discovered some three months later just below the peak holding a sketch that he'd done sitting on the summit of the previously unexplored mountain. It was posthumously named after him. The traditional inhabitants of the area called the peak Yarrawandangari which loosely translates to mean 'Stone where the white man sits' and is thought to indicate that they saw Baxter as he made his sketch, though some elders claim that the name goes back many generations.

As interesting as the information turned out to be Toby suspected the real reason they stopped was so his mother could catch up.

Toby was becoming impatient. Since they'd started their climb the itching on his birthmark had become almost unbearable

The track levelled off as they neared the wooden viewing platform built around the large rock that formed the peak. It was an unusual rock, different from all the other rocks that surrounded the area. It looked like it didn't belong, as though someone had placed it here for some mysterious purpose.

Toby walked around it. From the front it looked vaguely like a large old beaten up armchair. The effect was almost like someone had taken an armchair and then poured thick concrete over it which had set part way through the pour.

Toby looked at his birthmark. It was bright red and now throbbed as though with its own heartbeat. Without thinking, he reached out and pressed his palm against the rock. It felt cool, soothing and his itching stopped immediately. At the same time an ethereal voice spoke in his head. It recited the verse that Toby remembered from the scrolls:

For those who wish to take the seat
And make the crown their own
Then hand and sword must truly meet
And their blood be known

It was then that he knew he was connected to this rock in the same way that he was connected to Excalibur. But the voice continued:

When earth consumes the lesser light
Above the seat of stone
'Tis time to claim ones true birthright
And sit on Pendragon's throne

This was new. Toby could not recall that verse from anything he'd studied in Merlin's cave. He wished he had a piece of paper to write it down and hunted through his pockets. All he could find in them was a solid wad of a tissue formed no doubt by his habit of forgetting to empty his pockets before putting his clothes in the laundry basket. Asking for pen and paper would prompt too many questions, so instead he repeated the verse over and over to himself as he descended from the peak.

He must have been muttering out loud because his father pulled him aside as they reached the car.

"What's wrong?" he asked.

"Nothing," Toby replied.

"It's tomorrow isn't it?" his father said.

"Huh?"

"You were completely distracted for most of the way here, you almost ran up the mountain and now you've been talking to yourself all the way down."

Toby looked blankly at his father. His head was so busy remembering verse that he had no idea what his father was on about.

"I realise you're upset that we don't believe you.."

Then it clicked.

"But," his father continued "we don't understand why this boy is suddenly after you."

Toby switched mental gears and thought for a moment before replying: "It's not that sudden."

"Something happened at the school camp didn't it?" his father asked with a lot more insight that Toby gave him credit for.

Toby nodded "He's a bully and I began standing up to him a bit." He then related a couple of the incidents that occurred at camp and since, culminating in the chase down the lane to the sports field.

"Why aren't the teachers doing anything? Why are teachers like Mr Lloyd standing up for the boy?"

"Because he's good at footy!" The vehemence startled

his father.

He looked at Toby for a moment then placed a hand on his shoulder.

"I can only offer you one piece of advice son," he said gravely. "Tell the truth tomorrow and stick by it. The principal's a fair man and should give you a proper hearing.

"So you believe me then?" Toby asked.

"Let's just say that your version of events is sounding a lot more credible than it did."

It wasn't complete belief but it was the next best thing as far as Toby was concerned. He felt a tear welling in his eye and his father pulled him into hug. At that moment his mother arrived and eyed them curiously. His father gave her a look that said 'I'll explain later' and they piled into the car for the drive home.

◇◇◇◇◇◇

Toby explored the back seat for a pen or pencil. He would have even settled for a left over bit of crayon from the activity set that he'd had when he was little but there was nothing for him to write down the verses he'd heard on the peak. He sat back reciting the lines over and over in his head. The repetition combined with the gentle swaying soon sent Toby to sleep.

He was back on the peak. It was night and Toby could only just make out the silhouette of the odd shaped rock at the peak in the moonless darkness. He climbed the rock on the peak and with great ceremony sat down. Thunder rolled and there, suddenly was the full moon. A beam of light shot out from the moon, striking Toby and circling his head as though he was wearing a crown of light. There was a cracking noise and a bright flash of light and the rock broke away revealing a gold throne underneath. Time shifted and Toby was still seated on the gold throne but now it was in a great marble hall. Merlin was standing at his side. The hall was full of everyone he knew. They were all on their knees, heads bowed as though praying to him. The only exceptions were his parents sitting to one side looking immensely proud and Maguire and Mr Lloyd who were both in a cage at the back.

A guard opened the cage and dragged Maguire out and up the centre of the hall to the front were he was forced to kneel at the base of a stone block.

Toby stood and went to the side of the block. The guard bent Maguire over the block and pulled back his collar to expose the back of his neck. He lifted Excalibur high in the air, swung the blade down and …woke up.

They were still driving. Looking out of the windows he estimated they were roughly halfway home. He leaned back and closed his eyes in relief. The dream had seemed so real that his heart was still pounding. The pounding soon eased and he was almost drifting off again when his parents began talking to each other.

"I don't know," his mother said in answer to an unheard question from his father. "It's just he's been acting so odd lately."

"But that ties in to the whole school camp thing," his father argued. "If there was bullying going on it would be bound to make him act odd, particularly if no one was doing anything about it."

They drove in silence for a minute.

"Mr Lloyd mentioned the camp to me," his mother finally said. "Toby kept disappearing there for hours on end. No one could find him. And they suspected him of stealing food."

"Does that really sound like Toby?" his father asked.

"Well I wouldn't have thought so, but now…"

His mother left the statement hanging as they drove on in silence. Toby would have like to hear more but the rocking motion coupled with the fact that his eyes were closed, sent him back to sleep.

Chapter Twenty-Five

Toby arrived at school early, having been dropped off by his father on his way to work. His mother had insisted. He bridled at the lack of trust his mother was showing in him and was going to argue the point until he caught a look from his father that made him settle down. As a petty act of retaliation, he'd only given her a perfunctory peck on the cheek as a goodbye. Something his father berated him for on the way there. Not that he'd needed to, Toby had felt pretty bad the minute they'd left.

He stood alone in the playground, his stomach in a knot of tension. A lot of students looked at him from a distance but no one came over to speak to him. He spotted Brook looking his way. She gave him a tiny smile which, surprisingly, made him feel a lot better. She didn't come any closer though.

Billy arrived, his arm heavily bandaged, and Toby wondered if he actually had hurt him. He soon realised he hadn't, as Billy, when he thought no one was looking, used it to scratch his nose. Billy was soon joined by Warren and Maguire who both sneered at Toby but seemed happy enough to keep their distance.

Toby repeatedly touched the folded piece of paper with his detailed account of the incident. He'd gone over it so many times that he thought he'd remember it no matter how nervous he got but it was comforting to think that he could pull it out and read from it if necessary.

When Peter arrived he gave Toby a smile but kept as far away as he could, no doubt under a similar edict to Toby. Finally, the bell rang and he headed off to class. He only hoped that they'd call him to the principal's office early so he could get it out of the way and then, maybe his stomach might unclench enough so he could breathe properly.

◇◇◇◇◇◇

The first lesson started badly.

"Let's pick up where we left off last week shall we?" Mr Learer began, "Now who can tell me what we were up to?" Toby tried to make himself smaller. Don't pick me, don't pick me, he thought. "Toby?"

Toby mentally cursed. Normally he would be able to cast his mind back enough to remember something but for him 'Where we left off' was over three months ago and his mind came up blank. He scrabbled through his folder hoping he'd taken some sensible notes but all he could find were some meaningless doodles. He looked up helplessly and, thankfully, was saved from further embarrassment by a knock on the classroom door.

"Yes?" Mr Learer said, slightly annoyed by the interruption. The door slowly opened and a small head peered nervously around it. "Come in, come in." One of the boys whose lunch he'd saved came in clutching a note tightly in his hand. He gave Toby a grin of recognition as he handed the note to Mr Learer who immediately read it. He looked up. "Mr Cooper and Mr DeSilva, please report to the principal's office immediately.

Toby and Peter looked at each other. They both had a sinking feeling that they knew what this was about. Toby did a final reassuring check on his folded notes as he stood.

As they walked out Billy made a face at them and lifted his injured arm to give a little wave before dropping it back down and adopting the pained look he had been using all morning. The last thing they heard was Maguire sniggering as the door closed behind them.

◇◇◇◇◇◇

As Toby entered the principal's office, he was very surprised to see Mr Lloyd sitting behind the desk.

Mr Lloyd smiled at Toby but it wasn't a smile that had any warmth. It was more like the smile of a crocodile waiting to pounce on its prey. It broadened as Toby's face fell. His carefully prepared account was only good in a fair hearing and the chances of that weren't looking very good.

Mr Lloyd indicated a couple of chairs opposite him.

"I expect you're wondering why I'm here." Mr Lloyd asked as he opened up a folder in front of him.

They both nodded.

"Well as it happens Mr Hautler is on holidays and I am acting in his absence." He smiled again as Toby's hopes faded.

"Now, to this incident on Friday afternoon, I have their testimony in front of me and it's not pretty." Mr Lloyd said, relishing the obvious discomfort Toby and Peter were feeling. "According to this you both ganged up on poor little Billy Hays and were going to hurt him very badly if the others hadn't come along to stop you."

"But that's not how it happened," Toby protested. "The three of them were chasing me with sticks and I bumped into Peter and ..."

"I don't really care," Mr Lloyd said, cutting Toby off. "I choose to believe their version of events. After all Billy is the one nursing an injury."

There was a knock on the door. "Not now, I'm busy." The door opened despite his protest and Miss Sonnet apologetically entered.

"Miss Sonnet, I'm rather busy at the moment," he said indicating Toby and Peter. "So if you could come back later..."

"Oh but what I have to say relates to them," countered Miss Sonnet.

"Very well," Mr Lloyd sighed, waving his hand to indicate that she should continue.

"It's just that I witnessed the event last Friday that seems to have the whole school talking."

"What?" She definitely had his attention now.

"Well as you know, I like to unwind from the week with a little bit of Tai-Chi. A group of us regularly meet at the sports reserve every Friday afternoon.

With a flash of insight, Toby realised that the strange people he'd spotted on Friday were Miss Sonnet and her Tai-Chi group. Hope surged as she recounted the details of what she'd seen, confirming Toby and Peter's version of events and tearing Maguire's credibility to shreds. She concluded with, "It was a fine bit of, can I say swordsmanship – have you been training? – and if young Toby hadn't done what he did then I suspect that we would be visiting Peter here, in hospital."

Mr Lloyd sat back stunned. His plans for a long and arduous punishment, perhaps even suspension of Toby had crumbled, once again, to nothing.

"Very well," he said to both boys as he gathered himself as best as he could, "you may go."

They both stood and left the office, barely containing their relief.

"You will ring their parents and let them know won't you?" Miss Sonnet said just in that tone that meant if he didn't, she most certainly would. "I'm sure they'd be pleased to hear the whole story as it really happened."

"Of course I will," Mr Lloyd said through gritted teeth.

"Thank you," she said, as she smiled sweetly and followed the boys out.

◇◇◇◇◇◇

If Toby was expecting an apologetic mother that afternoon he was sadly disappointed.

She sat tight lipped and kept her eyes firmly ahead only glancing at Toby occasionally out of the corner of her eye.

Finally, Toby couldn't take it anymore.

"Did Mr Lloyd ring?" Toby asked.

"Yes," was his mother's abrupt reply.

Toby was confused. If Mr Lloyd had rung then his mother should now know the truth, unless…

"What did he say?"

His mother took a deep breath. "That there was provocation on both sides and while he didn't condone fighting he would let you off with a warning. He also said that it would be appropriate for us to decide a fit punishment for you."

Toby gaped. Once again the truth was nowhere to be seen. He sat in silence for a while.

"And what about Billy's mum?"

"His arm was only slightly bruised." And here his mother's voice took on a curious tone. "She said she didn't want to pursue it and that boys will be boys. I know if someone hit you with a tennis racquet I wouldn't be saying that unless…"

She continued to drive thoughtfully then looked at him properly for the first time that afternoon.

"You know," she added finally, "I'm beginning to come around to your father's way of thinking."

Toby smiled.

"Don't be too cheerful," she added, "I still want you home straight after school each day."

"And weekends?" Toby asked hopefully.

"We'll see." But she smiled as she said it.

Chapter Twenty-Six

Toby awoke with a start. He sat bolt upright, breathing heavily. It was still dark. Toby fumbled for his light then cursed as he remembered it was in several pieces. He hopped out of bed and padded across to the light switch. Toby squinted, allowing his eyes to adjust as bright light flooded the room.

What had panicked him? It must have been a dream, he thought. He vaguely recalled he was in class but it was being held on the top of a hill. He was supposed to recite a verse but couldn't remember the words... panic struck again. The verse. He thought he'd memorised it. Toby wracked his brain but couldn't remember the words of the verse he'd heard on the hill top.

If only he'd written them down that night, but there'd been the whole school thing happening and...

Making excuses to himself was pointless. He sat down at his desk and tried to remember the verse.

◇◇◇◇◇◇

The sun slowly crept above the horizon to find Toby, tired and cramped, still sitting at his desk though now he was surrounded by crumpled up bits of paper.

All he'd managed to remember was something about a light and Pendragon's throne but that was it. He stretched out and looked at his clock. There no point even thinking about bed. His alarm was due to go off in ten minutes. He yawned. It was going to be a long day.

A cold shower invigorated him enough to stay awake through breakfast during which a high level discussion by his parents decided it would be appropriate for Toby to walk to school today - not because he was back in the good books but more from the fact the school was completely out of the way for them to be dropping him off and picking him up.

After breakfast he left but with strict instructions to be home straight after school. The walk in the crisp morning air further cleared the muzziness from his head and by the time he arrived at school he almost felt normal.

◇◇◇◇◇◇◇

A sharp nudge to his ribs jolted him.

"Whaa..?" he looked around like a startled rabbit.

"You were asleep," Peter whispered. Toby blinked several times trying to focus. He was in geography and they were studying China and...

Another sharp nudge.

"What's wrong with you?"

"Didn't get much sleep last night," Toby replied stifling a yawn.

"Well you almost got caught," Peter whispered back.

Toby blinked several times and took a deep breath trying to clear the fog that had settled in his brain.

He focussed on what Mr Meridian, their geography teacher was saying. "The great wall is the only man made structure that can be seen from space and stretches from.... "

WHACK!

Toby jumped awake, his eyes wide open. Mr Meridian was standing next to him holding a metre long ruler that he had just slapped on to the desk in front of Toby.

"Sorry sir, but..."

"Principal's office, end of class," was the abrupt response to Toby's attempt at an explanation.

"Why didn't you warn me?" Toby whispered to Peter as Mr Meridian went back to the front.

"Wouldn't have mattered," Peter replied. "You were

snoring."

It was nearly dark as Toby trudged home. Mr Lloyd had taken great delight in issuing Toby a detention and even more delight in ringing his mother to inform her of the fact. Toby was dreading the reception he would receive when he got home.

As he walked up the street he noticed his father's car was parked in the drive. He was home early. Toby had a sinking feeling he was home early because of him. He was almost home when he noticed another car parked in the street in front. It was black. So black it seemed to suck the light from around it. Probably the reason Toby hadn't spotted it at first.

As he opened the front door, he could hear voices coming from the kitchen. Toby frowned. This was most unusual. Guests were always entertained in the lounge room. Only with family and close friends was his mother comfortable enough to allow them that far into the house.

He listened for a moment. The voice of his father and mother sounded normal. They were obviously chatting but their voice level was too low for Toby to make out any details. Then a third voice, a woman's, caused the pit of Toby's stomach to clench. There was also a hot sensation on his chest which he realised after a moment was coming from the sword, Excalibur which he had hanging there. Toby buttoned his shirt higher subconsciously hiding the sword. It was the voice of Morgiana

This is not good, he thought to himself. Part of him said, "run away" but another part knew that it's best to face your enemy. Summoning all his courage, he walked down the hall and opened the kitchen door.

Seated around the kitchen table were his mother, father and Morgiana. She rose as he approached.

"Aren't you going to say hello to your Aunty Fay?" his father greeted him and also began to stand.

Before Toby could say anything, she made a complicated gesture with her fingers and with a sweep of her arm, time stopped. His mother was frozen in the act of sipping from her tea, his father in the act of standing up, even the second hand on the kitchen clock was stationary. The only things seemingly unaffected by her spell was Toby and herself. Toby's stomach knotted.

"Give me the sword, boy?" She demanded as she took a menacing step forward. "I want it and I shall have it."

Toby stepped back. Excalibur flicked into his hand as he adopted a fighting stance.

"You can't take it from me," he said defiantly. "No one can."

She glared at him, her claw-like hand poised like a snake about to strike, her eyes flicking between him and the shining blade. There was greed in her eyes.

"Do not try to teach me the 'Lore of the Sword' impudent child," she snapped at him. "You shall hand it over to me."

"No I won't"

"Oh you won't want to but I assure you, you will."

Toby set his mouth firmly, readjusted his stance and glared at her.

Her laugh was pure evil.

She muttered something under her breath as her hand weaved around the heads of his parents. With a final flourish, the world resumed.

Toby quickly released Excalibur and it returned back around his neck.

"Well?" his father waited. He didn't seem to notice that Toby and Morgiana had moved.

"What?" said a confused Toby.

"Your Aunt Fay, aren't you going to say hello?"

"Oh don't embarrass the boy Henry," Morgiana said, patting his father on the arm, "I just wanted to ask him if he'd seen my necklace."

"Necklace?" his mother asked.

"Yes, it's a small amulet, shaped liked a sword. Toby was admiring it when you were visiting last week."

Had it only been a week? Toby ran through the days and was startled to realise that it had in fact been just over a week since his first encounter with Morgiana.

"And I haven't been able to find it since," she continued. "I was just hoping that Toby might remember where he last saw it." Morgiana smiled sweetly at them all. Toby felt the bottom fall out of his stomach. He realised what she was doing and there was nothing he could do about it.

"It's on a chain much like the one he's wearing now," she added.

"Toby doesn't wear a chain," his mother responded automatically.

Toby grinned triumphantly at Morgiana but she was not fazed.

"OH? I'm sure I caught a glimpse of one just before." Morgiana countered smoothly.

With a sigh, Toby's father placed a hand on his shoulder

"Come on Toby. Open your shirt and show your 'Aunt' that you haven't got her necklace."

"But... but..." Toby panicked. If only he'd mentioned the sword to them when he'd got back from camp. Even if he'd gone with the souvenir story, as pathetic as it was, he still wouldn't be in trouble now. He had to delay things.

"Come on Toby." His father said. Toby didn't, couldn't move. Impatiently he grabbed Toby's shirt and pulled it open.

There was a stunned silence as Excalibur, glowing brightly on the end of its chain, lay gleaming for all to see.

"Toby!" his mother said, dismayed. "Stealing?"

"But ..." Toby stammered.

"Please, please," 'Aunt' Fay interjected, "I only want

the amulet back. If he gives it back to me now, we'll put it down to the impetuous nature of youth and say no more about it."

"But ..." Toby stammered again.

"No excuses Toby. I am VERY disappointed in you," his father added. "Now it's time to start making amends Toby. I want you to give that amulet back to Aunt Fay and apologise. You can be thankful that she isn't going to take the matter any further."

Slowly, reluctantly he started removing the sword from around his neck. He hesitated, clutching it in his hands.

"Toby!" His father's voice was commanding and try as he might he could not bring himself to disobey.

Shaking with internal frustration, he proffered the sword to Morgiana. She snatched it and her eyes lit up in triumph.

"And the apology," his father demanded.

"Sorry," he said through gritted teeth.

"I knew deep down you were an honest boy," Morgiana said then added, whispering in his ear, "and it has been your downfall."

"Well I must be off." Her laugh though sounding normal, grated like nails on a blackboard. Toby was never sure if she left by the door or just vanished, his mind was in such a whirl. He'd lost Excalibur. The forces of chaos and evil had won.

He turned back to his parents who had resumed their spots at the table.

They both looked at him with disappointment.

"Two detentions, fighting and now this. What's going on Toby?" his dad asked

Toby had no answer. He wished they would yell at him but they just sat there calmly looking at him.

"I think you should go to your room," his mother finally said.

"But... but ..."

"Unless you have a good explanation for this then

I would suggest doing as your mother said for the moment."

Toby just stood there. He was in complete turmoil. Then it clicked. He was more worried about a sword than anything else. He had just upset his parents more than he ever had before and all he was worried about was a sword. The more he thought about it the more he realised that his problems all started since he'd found it. He was beginning to regret the day he'd ever laid eyes on it. He let out a sigh. There was nothing he could say that would set things right but he could make a start.

"I'm sorry," he mumbled as he turned and went out of the kitchen.

Chapter Twenty-Seven

Toby lay in the dark on top of his bed, unable to sleep. His parents had long ago gone to bed but not before his mother had brought him a sandwich and a drink to make up for the fact that he'd missed dinner. They sat untouched on his desk his stomach was too tight to even contemplate food.

Events kept playing over and over in his mind. Finding the cave, getting the sword, being attacked by Morgiana, the fight with Lothar, the numerous incidents with Maguire, the odd shaped rock on the hilltop, Morgiana making him hand over Excalibur, his parent's disappointed look, it all kept going around and around.

He must have drifted off at some stage because he was awoken by a knock on his door.

"Come in," he mumbled only half awake.

The only response was another knock.

"Come in," he said again, now fully awake.

Another knock but now he realised it wasn't coming from his bedroom door but rather his wardrobe. There was a faint glow coming from underneath the door that flickered slightly as he watched it.

Who or what could possibly be in his wardrobe? There were several suspects but Toby figured that if it was someone coming to attack him they were hardly likely to knock. That left only one candidate.

He got up and opened the door to reveal Merlin poised, ready to knock once more. He also noticed that his wardrobe was missing and he was now looking at a familiar sight, Merlin's cave.

"Thank the gods," Merlin said, relief flooding his face, "I was worried. I felt a powerful disturbance that does not bode well. Are you alright?"

"Couldn't be better," said Toby sarcastically.

"And Excalibur?" said Merlin completely missing Toby's tone.

"I gave it to Morgiana."

"Oh good," Merlin said before processing the answer. "WHAT?"

"I said I've given it to Morgiana."

Merlin grabbed Toby's shoulders; "What happened?" There was a look in Merlin's eye that Toby had not seen before, a desperate, fearful look. "Tell me what happened," he demanded. Toby struggled desperately against the druids tightening grasp. "YOU MUST TELL ME!"

"LET ME GO!" Startled by this outburst, Merlin lessened his grip slightly and Toby wrenched himself away and looked in terror at the druid.

"I'm sorry Toby, I…" Merlin looked in horror at his hands and at the expression on Toby's face.

"I think I'd better go," said Toby as he edged further away.

"No please," Merlin begged, "I need to know what happened."

Seeing the remorseful look on Merlin's face, Toby relented, he at least owed Merlin an explanation. He nodded and followed Merlin inside.

◇◇◇◇◇◇◇

"Just answer me one thing Toby," Merlin said as Toby finished, "Was Excalibur still hanging on its chain when you handed it over?"

"Yes."

Merlin breathed a sigh. "Then all is not lost. We still have time to find a way to get it back. Now first…"

"I don't want it back." Toby said this so quietly that Merlin seemed not to hear.

"…we need to find out where…"

175

"I don't want it back," he said louder.

Merlin sputtered to a stop. "You don't want it back?" he finally said.

"No."

Merlin stared at Toby his brow furrowed in concentration. Toby squirmed under the stare. It felt like Merlin's eyes were piercing through his head and reading the thoughts that lay underneath. There was a feeling of pressure building in his forehead. He tried fighting off the feeling but it only made it worse and the pressure turned to pain. Finally, he could take no more. "STOP IT!" The pressure eased and Merlin's face relaxed.

"I see you've made up your mind."

Tight-lipped, Toby nodded.

"May I ask why?" Merlin's tone was quiet but there was a hard edge to it.

Toby thought for a moment, trying to find a way of putting his feelings into words. Finally he said, "Ever since I met you, I've been in trouble with school and with my parents. I've even had people try to kill me and it's all because of this stupid sword. I've just had enough okay?"

"Then it is up to me to persuade you otherwise."

Merlin then proceeded to explain in detail why Toby should not give up. He mentioned that now Toby was no longer in possession of Excalibur and could no longer be the Pendragon, Morgiana and her cohorts would have a free hand to manipulate governments and business to do as they wished. He talked about the noble tradition of the Pendragon and how they have always stood for what is right and protected the weak and innocent. He passionately described how Toby's role was part of the prophecies and reminded him how he had already solved the riddle of one and was destined to figure out the meaning of the one about the seat (Toby almost gave away that he thought he'd already found it but successfully bit his tongue). Merlin finished by telling him that the fate of the world rested on his shoulders and they must act quickly before Morgiana figured out how to break the concealment spell.

"With you out of the way it will be bad," Merlin finished. "But if she manages to put Excalibur to use it will be infinitely worse."

Toby sat, arms folded, throughout the whole discourse. Several times he was almost swayed but each time he remembered the disappointed look on the faces of his parents and that strengthened his resolve.

"So, now we need to decide what to do next."

"I'm still not doing it."

Merlin appeared confused. "But I thought I..."

"NO!" Toby said. "I mean it. I've had enough. I want things back to normal."

Merlin's mood changed. He stood up to his full height, towering over Toby, and the cave dimmed.

"Things can never be normal for you again," he intoned ominously. "And you will stay here until you realise it."

"You can't keep me here," Toby snarled, "You can't control me. I remember that much of the prophecies, so don't even try!" And with that he stood up and strode purposefully out of the cave and back into his bedroom.

Merlin began to follow and this gave Toby the unique satisfaction of slamming his wardrobe door in Merlin's face.

Toby sat back on his bed and eyed his wardrobe door suspiciously. The glow still flickered slightly from underneath and Toby expected there to be a knock any second but after a few minutes the glow flicked out.

A moment later there was a soft knock. Toby's heart missed a beat until he realised it was his normal bedroom door this time.

"Come in," he said.

The door opened and his mother stuck her head around the door.

"Are you alright?" she said after flicking on the light and quickly scanning the room. "We heard a bang."

"Yes mum," he said, "I think I am."

She gave a half smile as if not fully understanding what he meant. "Goodnight then."

"Mum," he said before she could leave, "I know I haven't been myself lately, in fact ever since I got back from camp."

His mother came in fully and sat beside him on the bed.

"Your father and I have been very worried. We thought you may have been doing something silly."

Toby realised in horror what she meant. They thought he'd been doing drugs. No wonder they were worried. This just convinced him that he was well rid of Excalibur and all that it entailed.

"No mum it wasn't anything like that," he explained much to her relief, "I think it was more like an illness, something I picked up at camp but I'm over it now, I promise."

She gave him a hug and smiled. "You should probably sleep now."

Toby yawned and realised he was extremely tired.

"G'night mum."

"Good night." She kissed him on the forehead and tucked him in. He was asleep before she'd gone out the door.

Chapter Twenty-Eight

From that morning on things started to improve and every day that passed without incident seemed to help put his life back on to its old track.

The football team unsurprisingly finished the season on top of the ladder which gave them the luxury of a break before starting the finals series. Mr Lloyd however kept them even busier with extra training, the plus side of this being that Maguire didn't have time to cause him any grief.

Toby made a deliberate effort to avoid Maguire at other times and after two weeks they had hardly even glared at each other.

Alexis and Josh had been avoiding Toby since the school camp but they both began hanging around him again now that he was, in their words, acting a little less mental.

Peter agreed that he seemed more normal but as he had managed to win the local interschool tennis competition and progressed to the regional championships (an achievement that no one apart from Toby appeared even slightly interested in) he was spending even less time with Toby due to extra practice.

The one thing Toby did miss was sword training but he soon found a way to compensate. He made himself a training sword from an old broom stick with some lead sinkers attached to give it the right weight. If his parents thought it strange that he would spend hours out in the back yard attacking his old swing set, they never said anything. They just seemed pleased he was behaving normally the rest of the time.

After a few weeks it was as though none of the events involving Excalibur had ever happened.

Then little things started happening.

First was his bike. As he was now expected to go straight home, he'd taken to riding his bike to and from school. It started with a flat tyre, then both of them were let down, finally someone cut and bent his spokes making the bike unrideable. Two weeks of pocket money to fix it later, Toby decided enough was enough and went back to walking.

Next, his locker was broken into. He'd forgotten an assignment and had run back to the lockers between classes to grab it. Something niggled at him when he opened the door. Things just didn't seem right and it took a moment for Toby to realise that his books weren't how he left them. He quickly went through them all to see if anything was missing and that was when he'd found it, a watch that certainly wasn't his. He grabbed it and quickly shoved it in his pocket, making sure that no-one was watching. He then went and handed it in at the office, saying (quite truthfully) that he'd found it before rushing to class just in time to tell Peter what happened before the lesson started.

Mr Lloyd interrupted halfway through and announced that someone's watch had been stolen and there was going to be a locker search. They were all trooped out and Mr Lloyd made a great show opening each locker. He only gave each one a cursory glance until he got to Toby's. Here he grinned and pulled everything out, frowning as he emptied it. He went through the pile again giving Toby a piercing stare. Finally he glanced at Maguire who shrugged in confusion. The rest of the lockers were quickly done with no sign of the watch. Mr Lloyd announced they all had detention until the culprit owned up staring at Toby while he said it. It was then Peter piped up with the suggestion that it might have been handed in. Mr Lloyd was forced to admit that he hadn't checked and stormed off casting a furious glare at Maguire.

Toby tried to ignore all these incidents and keep telling himself that overall he'd made the right choice but there was still a nagging at the back of his mind.

Then Toby's nagging doubts became serious.

It started with a news bulletin. Toby had never really been interested in the news but it was always on in the background during their evening meal.

"This is unbelievable," his father said referring to a particular story that night, "I heard something about this on the radio."

His mother was about to say something but he shushed her and they turned their attention to the news.

The news reader had crossed to their US Correspondent who was now talking

"The recently passed changes to the first amendment come in to effect today. The change means the amendment no longer protects free speech if it has the potential to cause alarm.

"The impact from this is already being felt. FBI agents today swooped on the offices of National Geographic, seizing all information relating to its upcoming cover story on global warming."

The screen changed to a shot of the US President surrounded by advisors on the steps of the Whitehouse. "I will not allow the American people to be frightened by the extremist claims of a few radical environmentalists. Global warming is nothing more than a scare tactic designed to further destabilise the oil industry. Any threat to the oil industry, wherever it comes from, is a threat to our country and our people."

The scene changed back to the news reader who went onto another item.

They all sat there stunned: his mother and father by the story; Toby by the fact that, standing just behind the President, was Morgiana.

Toby watched the news intently for the next few days, he even read newspapers, but didn't see Morgiana again. He had just about convinced himself he'd been imagining things when he spotted a picture of the Prime Minister announcing that, in an effort to further stabilise the world oil market, several US oil companies were to be allowed to perform exploratory drilling on the Great Barrier Reef and there, in black and white, right at the edge of the photo, was Morgiana.

Merlin was right and the dark powers were rising. Toby knew he should do something. He knew he should find Merlin and do everything in his power to get Excalibur back but he couldn't.

Then one final incident galvanised him into action.

◇◇◇◇◇◇◇

It was the morning after the first round of the regional championships. Toby was eager to find out how Peter had done but by the time they had gone into their first class there was still no sign of him. About half way through the lesson the classroom door opened and Peter came in. He kept his back toward the class as he mumbled an apology to the teacher who, surprisingly, just gave him a sympathetic nod. He turned and headed for his desk and Toby could see his face properly.

He was horrified. Peter's left eye was completely swollen shut and there was a row of seven stitches across his eyebrow. The rest of the left side of his face was an angry shade of purple.

"What happened?" he whispered as Peter sat down next to him.

"Someone threw a rock at me." Peter winced several times as he spoke. "I had just won the match and was going to the net. Next thing I know I was in the dressing shed being patched up before going to the hospital for these," he said pointing to his stiches.

"Did anyone see anything?"

"No, but I found this in my sports bag this morning."

He brought a crumpled note out of his pocket.

Toby flattened it out. On it was scrawled 'That was for Billy and it's just for starters'.

"Maguire!" Toby muttered angrily.

◇◇◇◇◇◇◇

"I'm going to have it out with him," Toby said during lunch, after they'd spent the morning talking about it to each other - actually it was Toby who did most of the talking as Peter's face hurt too much.

"You're mad!" Peter said, wincing.

"Why is he mad?" asked Josh as he and Alexis joined them.

"He's going to take on Maguire. Oww," Peter said. This latest speaking effort seemed to have pulled a stitch.

"Was he responsible for that?" asked Alexis pointing at Peter's face.

Peter nodded. "Oww!" He stood. "Going to get some Panadol or something," he said and headed for the admin block. Toby distinctly heard Maguire snigger as Peter went past nursing his face.

Josh and Alexis looked at each other. "Mad!" they said in unison.

◇◇◇◇◇◇◇

Toby had no real plan in mind to deal with Maguire, just a vague idea that he'd follow him after school and tell him to back off. His only problem was he was still expected home straight after school but Toby thought he had the solution. Maguire would be held up by the additional football training so all Toby needed was an excuse to go back out again and Peter going home had given him that.

Toby raced home. He figured he had about a half hour up his sleeve to persuade his mother of his need to go back out. He told her about Peter and said he'd like to go over and see if he was okay.

"Well, let's ring," his mother suggested.

This was not what Toby was hoping for.

"He probably won't want to talk on the phone," he said after thinking quickly, "Besides I've got his homework."

"Alright," his mother finally agreed, "but don't be too long."

Toby nodded his agreement and was out the door before she could change her mind.

He ran furiously and quickly stopped at Peter's to fill him in before racing to the school just in time. Maguire, still in footy gear, came out of the gate and Toby drew back behind some bushes. Maguire didn't even look around. He headed straight up the road and Toby had no trouble following him.

Maguire turned a corner with a high fence and disappeared from sight. Toby ran up to the corner and peered around. Maguire had stopped and was talking to his father. Toby edged around a bit further and a feeling of cold dread went through him. There standing beside Maguire's father was Morgiana and next to her, Morton wearing Excalibur prominently around his neck.

He must have gasped out loud because something made Morgiana look his way. Her eyes narrowed and she made that same complicated movement.

The world froze apart from Morgiana, himself and interestingly Morton.

Toby tried to turn and run but was too late. Morgiana was upon him. She grabbed his shirt and hauled him around to face her.

"Well it's about time!" she said. "I was wondering what else I would have to do before you decided to come along."

Toby frowned. "So you've been making Maguire cause all the trouble at school?"

"But of course!" she said it so matter of fact. "It's amazing what a father will make his son do, particularly if he's in debt to me." So that was it. Toby remembered

184

the betting slips and figured somehow Morgiana was lending Maguire's father money so he could bet on the horses and claiming repayment in 'favours' instead of money. She must have had this planned for a long time and Toby wondered if Maguire was the way he was because of this.

"Why?" he said. "You've got what you want."

"Oh no," she sneered. "We want it all. We want the power of the Pendragon. Tell us how to release the sword and I'll leave you to your happy, if mundane existence."

So that was it. All he had to do was turn the sword back to full size and it would be over. Two weeks ago he would have jumped at the chance, even yesterday he would have considered it but now, after Peter, it wasn't even tempting.

"NO."

"Foolish boy!" she sneered. "Excalibur can't protect you now."

Her hand lashed out almost lightning fast and only Toby's reflexes, honed by months of training, saved him. He grabbed her wrist and held on. Morgiana was stronger than Toby but the shock of being held gave Toby a temporary advantage.

"I'd given up. I really had," he said as anger surged up through him. "But not any more. I am going to fight you." With that he pushed her back so she stumbled and fell, landing none too softly on her rump. Toby suppressed a grin.

Morgiana gestured and the world unfroze. "Get him!" she yelled. It took a moment for Maguire and his father to comprehend what was going on but they both started toward Toby. Even with his fighting skills, taking on someone the size of Maguire's father was something to be avoided. He turned and ran but not before seeing the tiniest flicker of concern in Morgiana's eye.

Chapter Twenty-Nine

Having decided to once again seek out Merlin, Toby resolved that this time he would do so in a way that wouldn't get him in trouble. This meant waiting until Saturday. It also meant avoiding Maguire for the rest of the week, a task that proved rather difficult.

Not a class went by without Maguire trying something to get Toby in trouble. It seemed like they were looking for any opportunity to put Toby in a position where they could intimidate him into doing what they wanted, or rather what Morgiana wanted. The worst was another attempt to frame him.

Toby had dropped a pen and it was only when he was straightening up he spotted something taped to the roof of his locker where he normally wouldn't see it. Toby pulled it out. It was a wallet. Toby was turning it over curiously when a voice came from behind him making him nearly jump through his skin.

"I'll hand it in for you. It will look suspicious if you do it again."

Toby spun around, his heart pounding.

It was Brook. "I don't know what he has against you but what he's doing is wrong."

Toby was at a loss for words.

"Here give it to me," she said, taking the wallet from Toby's unresisting hand.

"But...but they'll know you helped me," Toby stammered. "Won't they get back at you?"

"I don't care," she replied. "Since the school camp I've realised some things. And I, I ...I can't explain it but it's your fault!" She blushed, turned and ran off before a dazed Toby could say a word.

Toby requested a change of locker after that and made sure that he kept it a secret from Maguire.

◇◇◇◇◇◇

The weekend finally arrived and Toby told his parents, as casually as possible, that he was going for a bike ride. His recent good behaviour meant all he got was a "ride carefully, don't forget your helmet and be back in time for lunch."

He rode as quickly as he could to the spot he remembered the cave being and skidded to a halt. He could see no sign of Merlin's cave. Not too concerned, he ditched his bike and began searching the area in earnest. After half an hour he was scratched by trees, bitten by insects and still missing one cave.

He sat down and thought. He was definitely in the right place, he was sure of that. Perhaps he needed Excalibur? But the first time he'd found the cave was before he had the sword in his possession so it couldn't be that. Maybe if he really needed to find it, it would appear? But how could he do that?

Maybe if he meditated like he'd seen on TV and focused on the cave. It was worth a try. He sat crossed legged, as that was the only meditation pose that he knew of, and closed his eyes. He pictured in his head where he remembered the cave to be. He remembered what trees the path had led past and what rocks it had gone around. When he had that picture firmly in his mind, he opened his eyes. Relief flooded him as he saw the path leading to the cave.

Without hesitation he ran inside.

The cave was deserted. Everything was gone, the table, the chairs, even the fireplace. The cave was the same as when he first found it. He was too late. Merlin had given up too.

He looked around dejectedly at the barren cave remembering the strange shapes the rock formations made. The mother and child, the Rastafarians dreadlocks and the... that was it! The one that looked like an old man lying on his back on a bench. Toby went up to it and studied it in the dim light. There was no doubt. It was Merlin, cold and hard as stone.

"Merlin," he whispered. "Merlin," he said again placing his hand on the figures forehead, "I need you. Please!"

There was a cracking noise and faint colour began flowing into the figure. Toby stepped back as the figure lost the last of its stony appearance, sat up and looked expectantly at Toby.

There were many things that could have been said, apologies made, excuses given but he wouldn't have known where to begin, instead Toby stood straight up and looked Merlin in the eye.

"I'm ready! What do I have to do?"

◇◇◇◇◇◇◇

Merlin spent no time on recriminations. He busied himself and in no time the cave was the lived in haven Toby remembered. Merlin sat and almost seemed to snuggle into his seat.

"A lot more comfortable than a stone slab I can tell you," he said, noticing Toby's quizzical expression.

"Then why...?" Toby couldn't help but ask.

"For effect I suppose." Merlin replied after a moments thought. He indicated the other chair. "Now sit. There are things we must discuss."

And so they talked. They talked about losing Excalibur. They talked about Maguire. They talked about the news bulletins and the stories and what Morgiana might be planning next. They talked of the power Excalibur represented and how it must be used with care and responsibility and they talked of Morton and speculated how he fitted in to the scheme of things. At one point Merlin got up to replace the candles that had been new when they started but were now sputtering and Toby panicked. He'd probably missed lunch and now would be in trouble again. Merlin promised that he had the whole time thing sorted but Toby wasn't convinced until he'd gone back outside and seen for himself that the sun was still only half way up.

Calm once more he sat back down and they continued talking. The candles had burned halfway down again when Toby ended by telling of the last encounter he had with Morgiana and what he thought it meant.

Merlin tapped the ends of his fingers together and smiled as Toby finished.

"So she still hasn't managed to use it," Merlin said almost to himself, "Excellent."

"It must be a pretty powerful spell you put on it."

"Not really, it's just that it's tied to you."

"So they can never use it then," Toby said with relief.

"I didn't say that," Merlin replied. "If she put her mind to it and did a bit of research Morgiana could easily break it but," he added, "like most of her ilk she will go to extraordinary lengths to avoid anything that resembles hard work, a fact that we can hopefully use against them."

"How?"

Merlin folded his hands together and rested his chin (at least Toby assumed it was his chin, through the beard it was hard to tell) on his index fingers, which he'd left pointing up, and stared off into the fire, thinking.

After a minute or so he turned his gaze back to Toby.

"There may be a way," he said nodding to himself. "But it requires a few risks."

"What do I have to do?" Toby said without hesitation.

Merlin smiled but shook his head. "No Toby, I must do this," he said. "All you can do is be ready for when you are needed.

"When will that be?" Toby said eagerly. He felt he

had some catching up to do.

"That I cannot say, but it will be soon and I will find a way to contact you then. Now is there anything else you need to tell me?"

Toby thought for a moment before shaking his head. "Nothing that I can think of," he said and at that moment it was the truth.

"Then time for you to walk home me thinks"

"I rode"

Merlin raised his eyebrows, "I've never seen you with a horse."

Toby laughed. "It's a bike. A thing with two wheels that you ride," Toby added at Merlin's confused look.

"This I must see," Merlin said as he followed Toby out.

Outside, Toby picked up his bike and mounted it. Strapping on his helmet (another raised eyebrow) Toby said goodbye and rode off.

Chapter Thirty

The Sunday morning sun streamed through Toby's bedroom window. Toby lay there awake but revelling in the warm comfort of his bed. He had the best night sleep in ages due, in no small part, to having a totally free conscience for the first time in weeks.

Toby was already looking forward to seeing Merlin again and finding out what the plan was for him to get Excalibur back, but he knew it wouldn't be today even if Merlin did manage to get in touch. Last night his father announced that if it was fine they would definitely be going somewhere tomorrow. The blue sky outside meant that a trip was on and Toby wondered where they would be off to.

Then his stomach clenched in panic. He recalled the mountain and the extra verses of the prophecy that he couldn't remember. It was the one thing he'd needed to talk to Merlin about before he'd lost Excalibur and it had completely slipped his mind even when Merlin had asked if there was anything else.

Toby needed to speak to Merlin and tell him about it even though he couldn't remember the verse. With things the way they were, every bit of information was bound to be important. But it would have to wait until after today at least.

Then Toby had an idea.

◇◇◇◇◇◇

Toby waited until breakfast was nearing an end before seeing if his idea would work.

"Where are we going today?" he asked his father.

"Well..."

"Can we go back to that mountain?"

"Err... Which one?" His father was completely thrown by Toby's unexpected question."

"Yarrawandasomethingorother," Toby replied.

"Ah yes I remember that one, fascinating volcanic remnant if I recall. I guess we could revisit it," his father said looking questioningly at Toby's mother.

"Don't look at me," she said, "You're in charge of the expeditions."

"Then it's settled. Now run up and get ready."

Toby leapt the stairs two at a time. His plan was working. He dressed and grabbed a pocket notepad and a pen. This time he would be ready.

There was only one nagging fear. What if when he got there nothing happened? What if, now that he didn't have Excalibur, the stone on top was quiet? The possibility gnawed at him the entire way there and all the way through lunch, which was thankfully just some sandwiches and fruit that he managed to force down.

When lunch was finished Toby scrambled his way up the hill leaving his rather bemused parents behind. The summit was deserted. Toby took a deep breath and pressed his hand against the stone. Warmth spread up his arm and the same ethereal voice spoke in his head, repeating the verses.

For those who wish to take the seat
And make the crown their own
Then hand and sword must truly meet
And their blood be known
When earth consumes the lesser light
Above the seat of stone
'Tis time to claim ones true birthright
And sit on Pendragon's throne

Toby quickly pulled out his notepad and wrote the second verse down. He also wrote down the name of the place and did a quick sketch just in case they were also important. Pleased with himself and breathing a sigh of relief Toby put away his notepad, closed his eyes and leaned against the stone.

The warmth from the stone radiated through his back and the voice, if anything, was louder – it also had pictures.

It was like he was in a dream watching but not really there. First there was Cadbury Tor. The gates were open and a troop of guards rode in led by a young warrior. At their centre rode a lady. Every now and then the warrior turned and looked back at the lady and they shared a smile. Toby instinctively knew the lady was Guinevere but he didn't know who the warrior was, even though it felt important.

The scene blurred to the great hall decked out with garlands and banners. Arthur and Guinevere were standing before Merlin at the head of the hall and Toby realised they were being married. The scene blurred once more. Arthur was seated on a bed. Guinevere approached and embraced him, only it wasn't Guinevere. Toby sensed the magic, he saw through the illusion to see Morgiana kissing Arthur. It made Toby squirm.

Again the scene blurred and showed Morgiana holding a baby. The baby grew until it was a boy about Toby's age. The boy looked disturbingly familiar then he changed to another boy and another each familiar and yet different from the last until the final change and Toby recognised Morton. Morton was descended from Arthur too, Toby realised, but through Morgiana and her trickery. Toby barely had time to comprehend this when the scene changed once more.

He watched as a troop of horsemen rode grimly by. Arthur was at their head followed by Bors, Cador, Hector, Bhadvere and Caedmon. Another figure also looked familiar but Toby couldn't quite place him. Then he realised it was Caleb, only about fifteen years older than when he'd last seen him.

Another change and the riders had now pulled up

to a halt facing Morgiana's boy on a horse. Arrayed behind him was a horde of hooded warriors. Arthur and the boy appeared to be talking but then the boy threw his head back in a wicked laugh and the scene blurred.

Battle was raging all around. Excalibur flashed in the sunlight as Arthur hacked away at the hooded foes. But for every one he despatched it seemed several took his place. Hector fell, then Bors. The battle was not going well. Caleb was also fighting several opponents at once. He had matured into a fine swordsman and was easily holding his own. Then one hooded warrior got behind him. Toby's heart leapt to his throat as the warrior swung his axe and it bit deep into Caleb's back. He went down leaving only Arthur and Bhadvere facing the horde and the scene blurred again.

Arthur lay in a pool of blood, he was alive but obviously weakened though he still had Excalibur gripped firmly in his hand. The boy strode triumphantly up to Arthur but now he was accompanied by Morgiana. She laughed and with a wave of her hand the remaining horde faded to nothing. At that moment Toby hated her more than ever before. She had created those beings that had killed his friend.

She spoke to Arthur and held her hand out expectantly but Arthur shook his head and tightened his grip on Excalibur. She screamed at him but he denied her again. She lunged forward but was stopped by an invisible force and could get no closer to him. She snarled something, grabbed the boy and walked off. As she left, a snake crawled out from the undergrowth. Arthur didn't see it until it was too late. It sank it's fangs into his leg and the scene blurred once more.

Arthur was now lying beside a lake being nursed by Bhadvere. Arthur was fading rapidly but kept whispering something to Bhadvere who kept shaking his head. Finally Bhadvere agreed and took Excalibur out of Arthur's unprotesting fingers. He struggled up and after a moments hesitation flung the sword out into the lake. The scene faded to black and Toby lurched away from the rock as though pushed. He opened his eyes just in time to see his father arrive at the summit.

◇◇◇◇◇◇◇

The images he'd seen while leaning against the rock preoccupied him all the way home. Particularly disturbing had been witnessing the death of his friend Caleb. Rationally he knew that Caleb had died over a thousand years ago but seeing it like that was hard.

Toby barely noticed when they arrived home. He roused himself enough to go inside and flop on the couch where he sat staring off into space. Thankfully his parents just thought he'd worn himself out running up the hill and didn't bother him.

After an hour though his mother came in and sat next to him.

"You all right?" she asked.

Toby nodded but only half heartedly.

"Is something troubling you?"

Toby responded with an unconvincing shake of the head.

"Then you shouldn't be stuck inside. There are still a couple of hours of daylight left. Why don't you go for a ride on your bike?"

Like mothers throughout the ages, his had instinctively suggested the one thing that would help. He did need to get out and clear his head and a long bike ride was just the thing to do it.

Chapter Thirty-One

The bike chain clanked as Toby changed gears down. This bit of the road was always the hardest part but only rarely did Toby give in to the temptation of getting off and pushing. It was a challenge he set himself every time he rode up here.

The hills behind Middle Park were undeveloped. It was almost like being in a different country. They created a natural barrier to the urban sprawl; one side suburbia and the other a rural setting where he was more likely to see a cow than a car.

With a final few pedals he reached a level section that ran for a hundred metres or so before the final rise to the top. He pulled off the road and stopped. Here there was a small unofficial lookout, no more than a wide bit of verge that took advantage of a gap in the trees allowing for a view of the valley below and the river snaking through it, a sight that was obscured at the official one at the top. Toby often came up here to think or just to take in the view. Often he would just sit and stare, his mind on nothing in particular but sometimes he'd close his eyes and imagine there was a village down in the valley. In his mind's eye he would see the stone cottages with wisps of smoke rising from their chimneys, the inn with its crowds and ruddy faced innkeeper and hustle and bustle of the market square.

Today though there was no need.

It wasn't exactly how he'd imagined it, the cottages seemed to be made of wood, he couldn't seem to spot an inn of any description but there could be no doubt that there was now a small village nestled on the other side of the river.

There was only one thing to do. Toby hid his bike in some bushes and made his way down through the gap into the valley below.

As Toby crossed the bridge and approached the village, the first building he came to was a smithy. Several horses were lined up waiting for the attention of the blacksmith who looked up from his anvil as Toby approached.

"Greetings lad" the blacksmith hailed him.

"Hi."

The Blacksmith raised an eyebrow at this greeting and picked up the horseshoe he was working on with a pair of tongs.

"You'll be wanting the hall of justice I'd imagine," the blacksmith said.

"Will I?"

"Aye," the blacksmith replied as he plunged the shoe into a barrel of water and briefly disappeared in the ensuing cloud of steam. "'Tis the only reason you could be here."

Toby had no idea why he was here, so going to the hall of justice sounded like a good idea.

"Where is it?" Toby asked.

"The far end of the village," the blacksmith replied as he came out to the horses. "'Tis the only stone building. You can't miss it"

"Thank you."

"Here." The blacksmith handed Toby the still warm horseshoe.

Toby took it, not quite sure what to do with it though.

"For luck," the blacksmith explained. "Keep it close to you but out of sight."

Toby pulled his t-shirt up and shoved the horseshoe in the waistband at the back of his jeans, letting his t-shirt drop back over it.

"Thank you," Toby said sincerely.

The blacksmith peered intently at Toby for a moment then slapped him on the back.

"I think you'll do lad," he said. "Aye I think you'll do."

The hall of justice was indeed the only stone building in the village. It was mainly sandstone with granite corners and marble pillars out front. The overall appearance could at best, be described as having a "unique character". To Toby's mind, it was just plain ugly.

With a shrug, he approached the large oak doors, grabbed the iron handles and opened them.

The inside was one large courtroom, almost church like in its design. It was packed with all manner of people although 'people' was being generous in describing some of the occupants of the benches that filled the gallery of the court. The bailiff, a small balding man, again 'man' was generous as most men don't have pointy ears and tend not to wear curly toed shoes, glared at Toby and waved him toward a seat.

Toby slid on to a pew and found himself seated next to a small man with a full beard.

"Hello"

"You're one of the little people?"

"Don't be daft! I'm a dwarf and fiercely proud of it."

"Sorry. I didn't mean any offence."

"None taken."

They sat in silence for a moment. "My name's Toby."

"Colin," the dwarf responded.

"Colin!"

"Aye," he sighed. "That's why I'm here. I'm petitioning to change my name to something a bit more dwarvish."

"Order! Order!" The judge banged his gavel and a roll of thunder filled the chamber. Toby suspected that the gavel wasn't quite normal either.

The judge took a scroll in each hand and held them out as though comparing their weight.

"Hmmm," the judge pondered. "I think I'm ready to make a judgment."

Toby watched totally fascinated by the fact the judge hadn't actually read either of the scrolls.

"I have weighed the merits of each case and therefore find for the plaintiff"

"Case adjourned"

There was a general hubbub of discussion as the next group made their way to the well of the court. Colin nodded his head. "Good decision," he added.

"But he didn't even read the evidence."

"Why would he want to read it?" Colin said, "It would just be confusin'. No, he's far better just weighin' the evidence like we saw."

"But he was just holding the scrolls."

"Aye," said Colin respectfully. "He's very even handed."

Toby was prevented from pursuing the point any further by a touch at his elbow. He turned to see Merlin sitting there next to him.

Relief flooded through Toby. He hadn't realised how tense and worried he'd been.

"Well met my young friend," Merlin said as he settled himself, "I believe we will be called shortly."

"Why are we here? Actually, where is here?"

"We are in the land between the faerie realm and yours."

Toby forced back the desire to laugh. "Fairies?"

"Faeries," Merlin corrected. "Their realm lies alongside yours but separated. Occasionally the barrier between weakens and glimpses can be seen. That is why your history is full of stories and creatures that only truly exist there."

"Like a parallel universe," Toby observed thinking of some of the episodes of Star Trek he'd watched (mostly at his father's insistence).

"Er yes," said Merlin seemingly surprised at Toby's grasp of the concept.

"And this place you said it was in between?"

"The two cannot meet, that would be disastrous, but there are locations where the barrier is always weak. So this place exists as a kind of common ground. A meeting place between the worlds and, more importantly, a neutral area where those in conflict can meet and attempt to sort out their differences."

"So you got Morgiana to agree to solve things here with him?" Toby said indicating the judge.

"Not exactly," and would say no more as the next case had started and they were ordered to silence.

Chapter Thirty-Two

Toby sat through several more cases, all following the pattern of the last. Each side would present a scroll which the judge would pick up and weigh in his hands. He would then deliver a verdict.

Nobody seemed to be upset by the results but Toby was becoming increasingly nervous. Finally their turn came and they approached the front of the court.

Morgiana approached at the same time along with Morton who was still prominently wearing Excalibur and smirking at Toby.

The bailiff, a small man that Toby suspected was also a dwarf, rose and read out the details of the case.

"The plaintiff, Morgiana also known as Morgan La Fey hereby petitions this court to issue an order requiring the defendant, one Toby Cooper, to remove a spell that prevents them from using Excalibur, it being freely given to her under and according to ancient lore."

Toby was startled. Morgiana had taken this action, not them. Merlin placed a hand on Toby's shoulder and whispered; "This is part of the plan."

"And that all parties agree to be bound by the decision of this court in this realm and the next?" The dwarf finished and Toby found himself nodding along with Merlin, Morgiana and Morton.

"Hand me the scrolls." The judge held his hands out expectantly.

"Your Honour, we request to present our case verbally and call a witness."

The judge raised an eyebrow. "Highly unusual request."

"But not without precedent," Merlin argued

"Your Honour," Morgiana interrupted. "Merlin is merely trying to waste time. Everyone knows the methods of the hall of justice and if he is too old and lazy to have prepared his case then it deserves to be thrown out."

Merlin pulled a scroll out of his robe. "I have prepared my case as per convention but in preparing it I felt that this was one of those rare occasions where the written word will not get us to the truth. "Particularly," he added, "as we dispute their right of ownership."

"What?" Morgiana screeched. "You tricked us into coming here you lying scheming rodent."

BANG!

The judge's gavel sent a roll of thunder through the room.

"Very well I shall hear the evidence and resolve ownership before going any further."

They all went to nearby tables where they sat. All except Morgiana who stood fuming.

"I insist," she said through clenched teeth, "that if we must go through a dispute on its ownership, at least let the sword be in its true form."

The judge nodded in agreement and looked expectantly at Toby.

He went over to Morton and took the necklace from him, held his hand up and focused. A wave of muttering spread through the court as Excalibur appeared in his hand. If he ran now.... but how far would he get he didn't even know how to get back to his world. With a sigh he reluctantly handed Excalibur back to Morton and returned to his seat.

Morton gave Morgiana a knowing smirk but it was short lived as the judge spoke.

"In the needs of fairness the sword should be placed here on the bench until its fate is decided."

Morgiana looked decidedly unhappy as Morton sulkily placed Excalibur on the bench in front of the judge.

"Now who is this witness you wish to call?" asked the judge.

"I call Toby Cooper," Merlin said to Toby's surprise.

He stood nervously but Merlin said, "Have faith young Toby. If you present the truth, the absolute truth, then we will win," and ushered him forward.

The dwarf produced a stool and placed it near the bench. Toby gathered he was meant to sit on it.

Once settled the judge leaned forward toward Toby. "I gather it is customary where you come from to swear on a book of some description, a religious text I believe. Do you require this?"

"No," Toby replied. "But I promise to tell the truth."

The judge gave him a penetrating stare before saying, "It appears that you do. Who wishes to question him first?"

Merlin bowed toward Morgiana indicating that she could and she smiled nastily and turned her attention to Toby.

"I have one simple question to ask of you," she began. "Did you give Excalibur to me?"

Toby was immediately faced with a dilemma. If he said no then they might win but he would have lied. But it was sort of true though because he hadn't wanted to give it so...

"Well?"

The truth. The absolute truth. That's what Merlin had said. The absolute truth.

"Yes, I did." Toby answered. The court erupted. Morgiana looked highly pleased and the judge had to bang his gavel sending several rolls of thunder through the court before everything quietened down.

"In light of this answer I would respectfully request that our right of ownership is proven under the ancient lore."

The judge looked questioningly at Merlin who slowly rose to his feet.

"If I may be permitted to ask some questions to clarify that answer, Your Honour?"

The judge nodded his permission.

"Toby," Merlin began. "Did you want to give it to her?"

"No."

"Then why did you?"

"Because my parents asked me to"

"And why did they ask you to Toby?"

"Because they thought I had stolen it from her and the right thing to do would be to give it back." Toby replied miserably as the memory of this came back.

"What gave them the idea it was stolen?"

"She told them it was hers."

Another ripple of muttering went around the courtroom but stopped before the judge needed his gavel again. Morgiana jumped up.

"He gave it to me willingly."

"But he didn't want to, I wouldn't call that willing unless you are aware of some new definition of the word," Merlin responded

"The Lore states…" Morgiana began but was cut off

"Enough!" the judge said as another roll of thunder echoed through the chamber. "Unless there is more testimony…" He looked expectantly at both of them. "Then I shall now decide ownership."

With that the judge held his hands out flat, palms facing up.

At first Toby couldn't see anything but after a moment each palm held a speck of light. The specks grew until the left held an angry ball of red light with black marbling running through it about the size of a golf ball. The right was a basketball sized ball of pure dazzling white.

The judge closed his hands and the balls vanished.

"I have weighed the evidence. And find that Toby did voluntarily hand over Excalibur according to the letter of the Lore." Morgiana looked triumphant and Toby's heart sank but the judge hadn't finished. "But not the spirit and it is the spirit by which I shall judge."

"But the Lore..." Morgiana protested

"Don't quote the Lore to me," the judge thundered. "Are you forgetting who wrote it?"

Morgiana quietened.

"You have spent too long in a place where they hold the letter of their law above the spirit in which it was made and it shows in your tricky manipulation of him and his parents. You put him in the unenviable position of either giving you the sword which he knew was wrong or disobeying his parents which he knew was also wrong. That he chose to give you Excalibur rather than disobey his parents shows how much he loves them and I commend him for that." He leaned over and peered intensely at Morgiana who was not looking at all happy. "That you made his parents believe that their son was a thief is not so commendable and as part of my judgement I demand that you correct that belief."

The judge straightened and addressed the court. "I find that the true owner of Excalibur is Toby Cooper further I find that this negates the cause for the petition to remove enchantment so I therefore dismiss the petition."

There was a level of pleased muttering.

"Toby," the judge said. "You may come and claim Excalibur."

Morgiana's face clouded in anger and she snapped.

"No!" she screamed and made a desperate lunge for Excalibur.

The judge banged his gavel but this time rather than a roll of thunder, a bolt of lightning shot out of it, striking Morgiana on her chest and pushing her back so that she landed unceremoniously on her rump.

Her face twisted in rage and she thrust her hand out. There was a crackle of energy and a ball of flame appeared in her palm. She flung it straight at Toby. It hit him squarely in the back and....

Vanished.

There was a gasp of astonishment from the onlookers. None were more surprised than Morgiana. Toby had felt nothing more than a slight warmth. Toby reached around to his back to feel the warm spot. His fingers instead found the metal shape of the horseshoe. He'd forgotten about it. "For luck" the smith had said. Well it had obviously worked, and now Toby couldn't help but grin at the look on Morgiana's faced as she tried to comprehend what happened.

The judge seemed almost amused too. "Normally that would have attracted a rather hefty penalty," the judge observed. "But as your intended victim has not been harmed by your attack I will let him determine what your penalty is."

Morgiana struggled to get up and protest but the judge raised his gavel once more in readiness.

She slumped and looked at Toby venomously. Toby briefly considered suggesting some form of outlandish punishment but after a moments thought decided against it. Instead he just shrugged. "It's not worth worrying about," he said finally.

The judge nodded. "So be it. You should be grateful to this young man. He has shown wisdom beyond his years."

Morgiana's face twisted again and she looked about ready to attack once more but Morton whispered something in her ear and she calmed down. She stood and composed herself. "My apologies for that outburst," she said as she gave the judge a slight bow. "I shall of course accept and abide by the decisions of the court." She turned and walked out, Morton following just behind. Toby thought he detected just the hint of a smile on her face as she walked past him.

Toby took Excalibur and was about to return it to its place around his neck but Merlin stopped him.

"Leave it out. Carry it as we leave."

Toby shrugged and followed Merlin out as the judge called for the next case.

◇◇◇◇◇◇◇

A crowd waited outside the hall. Toby squinted as he emerged from the inside, surprised to see so many people. He wondered what they were doing there. Excalibur gleamed in the bright sun, dazzling the gathered crowd.

One or two people began to clap. More followed and soon the crowd were cheering madly.

"What are they cheering at?" Toby asked.

"Why you of course," Merlin replied.

"Why? I haven't done anything."

"And telling the truth even when you thought that telling a lie would be better is nothing?" Merlin said. "They know who you are and what you stand for and that is what they are applauding."

"But..."

"Shssh! Hold Excalibur up."

Toby did as instructed and the crowd quietened as Excalibur glowed in the sun bathing the whole village in its ethereal light.

"Now put it away," Merlin whispered and Toby released Excalibur It vanished and Toby immediately felt its comforting presence around his neck once more. He was still the centre of attention of the now quiet crowd and he began to feel slightly foolish. He didn't know what made him but he bowed to the crowd. As one, they bowed back then all stepped back or to the side to make a pathway for him. Merlin patted his back.

"Time to go," he said as he led off giving Toby no choice but to go after him. The crowd closed in behind them as they passed and followed them as they wove their way through the village.

They stopped following at the bridge and Toby realised this was the boundary and they couldn't follow any further. He turned to have one final look at the village and caught the eye of the blacksmith he had met on the way in. The blacksmith gave him a nod as though in approval and Toby smiled, removing the horseshoe that had saved him and holding it to his chest as a salute. With a final smile at the crowd he turned and crossed the bridge feeling a slight tingle as he did so.

Once on the other side Toby looked back once more but was not surprised to see nothing but an empty field stretching out behind him.

"I will walk with you to your contraption," said Merlin.

Merlin regaled him of how he'd managed to get Morgiana to not only agree to be heard in the court but suggest it herself in the first place.

"It was easy, once I'd said that the only way I'd get you to remove the enchantment were if you were ordered to by the court. I knew she couldn't resist the bait of an easy outcome."

Merlin remained in a cheerful mood until they neared where Toby left his bike. He turned and laid his hands on Toby's shoulders.

"Toby," he began solemnly. "Today was a victory of sorts but it was not the final battle. That is still to come and as soon as we can decipher the meaning of the verse we shall know what we face."

Then Toby remembered. "Two verses," Toby said.

"Hmmm?" said Merlin only half paying attention to Toby.

"There's another verse."

Merlin looked as Toby at though he'd grown an extra head. "Then I think you'd better tell me about it," he finally said.

Chapter Thirty-Three

As they walked, Toby related what he had experienced at the mountain. He choked up a bit when it came to the images of the battle and Merlin laid a comforting hand on his shoulder. For the first time he thought about what it must be like for Merlin to have left everyone else behind and he realised how little he really knew about Merlin. He made a mental promise to himself that he would try and be a friend to Merlin if he wanted him to be.

"We will have time for sentimentality later," Merlin said as though having just read his mind. "Your vision answers many question, particularly about the boy."

"What about the warrior with Guinevere?" Toby asked. "He seemed important."

"Indeed," said Merlin. "His name is Lansaighalán."

Toby furrowed his brow. The name meant nothing.

"It loosely translates to Lancelot."

"Oh," was all Toby could think of saying.

"Enough of that for the time being," Merlin said. "You must focus on completing the prophecy now that we have a fair idea of what is required."

"Do we?" asked Toby, "I thought all we really knew was where the seat of stone was."

"More than that young Toby, much more than that," Merlin explained. "Firstly, the stone you discovered is the ancient throne of the Pendragon and is the seat referred to in the first line. This is confirmed by line four of the second verse"

Toby looked sceptically at Merlin. "Look I know I've seen a lot of weird stuff but how can the ancient throne of King Arthur be half way round the world from where he lived?"

Merlin shrugged. "It's like my cave. It turns up where it's needed. If you lived in Africa or Siberia it would be there too."

"Secondly," he continued, "Only you can sit there."

"How do you know that?"

"For those who wish to take the seat
And make the crown their own
Then hand and sword must truly meet
And their blood be known"

Merlin recited. "That can only refer to you. How many others of the Pendragon bloodline do you know that currently possess Excalibur?"

Toby had no answer for that so Merlin pressed on.

"Finally, when you sit there you will be crowned."

"And what does that mean?"

"You will be the Pendragon," said Merlin, surprised at the question.

"And what does that mean?" repeated Toby.

Merlin stopped. "Why, I thought you knew lad." Toby shook his head.

"So everything you've done, the struggles, the training, you did it all without knowing why?"

Toby shrugged. "I just thought that...that..."

"My boy, all this is leading to one final thing, claiming the throne and the crown of the Pendragon and that means you will be king."

"King?" Toby said sceptically. "King of what?"

"Why - everything," Merlin replied.

"You mean..."

"The whole world. Everything. All people will bow before you acknowledging the birthright handed down over the ages. You will be the king."

King! The thought of it made him stop in his tracks. King! It didn't make sense... and yet it did. It was little things, the way people had treated him recently, the way that some of them had looked to him for help and then there was all the old scrolls and Merlin himself. He hadn't thought about it but here was history's most famous wizard and he was standing not a metre away.

King! The dream he'd had in the car after finding the rock. He'd been king in that and it had been ... he shuddered as he recalled how the dream had ended.

King...

"Not sure I want to be king," Toby finally said.

"Good," Merlin said to Toby's surprise and then added. "Those that crave power are often those that are least likely to use it well."

Merlin took in a deep breath.

"I can feel it Toby. The time is closing in. 'When Earth consumes the lesser light' that sounds like a time to me. Any thoughts as to what it means? "

Toby had none.

"Never mind," Merlin continued more cheerfully than Toby would have expected, "I'm sure the answer will make itself evident in good time and we will discover 'the when'. I suspect though that time will be soon."

As they parted ways that afternoon Merlin's mood was upbeat. Toby, however, had a niggle at the back of his mind that he couldn't put a finger on. It might be the memory of his dream as the whole thought of being king made him nervous. It might be the sense of urgency he felt about 'the When' particular as Merlin made it sound like it could be any minute. It could be any number of things. Toby wasn't sure, but something they had discussed that afternoon was pulling a little rope labelled 'Niggle'.

◇◇◇◇◇◇◇

Toby could not stop trying to figure out what was niggling and he kept coming back to 'the when'. He still couldn't make head nor tail of the line 'When earth consumes the lesser light'. He'd racked his brain trying to figure it out. Even though, still unsure if the final outcome was what he wanted, he did want it over. He kept rolling the line around in his head "When earth consumes the lesser light." it obviously referred to a time but no matter how hard he tried he couldn't figure it out.

Over the next few days he was so preoccupied that his parents noticed, particularly when he appeared to be staring off into space during the middle of his favourite TV show.

"Anything wrong?" his mother asked as he sat there, oblivious to the fact that the show's hero was now hanging from a low branch in the middle of a river surrounded by hungry crocodiles.

"Just trying to figure something out," he said without thinking. "For a school project," he added quickly after seeing a look of concern appear on his mothers face.

"Why not look it up at the library?" she suggested.

The simplicity of the suggestion startled Toby. The library. Even if they didn't have a book about it specifically he could use one of the internet terminals there. Toby was not allowed to use the internet access at home since he'd accidentally run a virus infected program that had wiped out several weeks of his father's work the year before. He mentally berated himself for not thinking of the library himself.

"Great idea mum, I'll go tomorrow after school," he said gratefully and turned his attention to his show.

◇◇◇◇◇◇

The library held a surprise for Toby. When he arrived, he sat at the last free terminal, took out his notepad and then discovered Brook seated at the terminal next to him.

"What you doing?" she inquired.

"Uh just some research," he replied vaguely. "You?

"History assignment," she said with a look on her face that said she'd not only rather suck lemons, but had been practising.

They chatted about all sorts of things and time just slipped away until Toby looked up at the clock and realised why the assistant librarian had been coughing increasingly louder for the last couple of minutes. It was almost half past and the library was due to close. They gave each other a guilty grin as they realised neither of them had done anything but talk. Toby picked up his notepad, putting it safely in his top pocket and left the library with Brook. The rest of the school buildings appeared deserted. Only the admin block looked busy but then the library lights flicked out leaving only the staff room and principal's office still with light shining from behind the venetian blinds that seemed to be compulsory fittings in all the admin buildings. There was one area though that was still a hive of activity. The oval.

Mr Lloyd had been running a lot of extra training for the football team in the run up to their finals match and tonight was no exception. Toby briefly debated going out another way but Brook had no hesitation in heading that way. Toby decided he wanted to spend a bit more time with her and avoiding the oval just seemed silly so he headed off with her.

They had barely passed where Mr Lloyd was standing on the sidelines when Toby heard the footsteps running behind him. He braced himself but the impact still sent him tumbling down to the ground. Before he could begin to pick himself up a weight landed on his back pinning him. He struggled trying to see who was tackling him but the first weight was joined by another. He was helpless

"Hold him down."

He wasn't surprised to hear Maguire's voice, just angry. He must have been in full view of Mr Lloyd but as usual Mr Lloyd wasn't going to do a thing and that made him angrier. Toby felt a hand fumbling at his collar. It grabbed the chain holding Excalibur and looped it off Toby's neck.

"Got it!" he heard Maguire say followed by footsteps running off.

"What is going on there!" it was a shrill feminine voice that called out.

"Errr yes, stop that!" Mr Lloyd's voice joined in.

Suddenly he was free. He rolled over in time to make out Warren and Billy running off around the corner. He got to his feet to see who had intervened and was only slightly surprised to see Miss Sonnet charging across the field to Mr Lloyd. He also noticed there was no sign of Brook.

She set me up he thought furiously.

"What were you thinking?" Miss Sonnet demanded of Mr Lloyd as she approached.

"I only noticed them myself when you called," Mr Lloyd said.

"Rubbish," she said scornfully. "You were watching the whole thing and doing nothing. I am going to have to report you."

"Try it," he sneered. "No one is going to believe you."

"Oh I think they will," said a new voice and they all turned to see the principal, Mr Hautler, striding towards them.

"Go home, but report to my office in the morning please," he said to Toby before turning his attention to Mr Lloyd. "And as for you, my office, now!"

Toby left and ran to the gates, anger still burning in his stomach. He didn't know what to do. He wanted to kick something in frustration but one clear thought cut through the angry haze. Maguire had Excalibur. Getting it back had to be first. Toby took a calming deep breath. Maguire was long gone and Excalibur with him but there was a feeling. He turned around. It almost felt like there was a thread tied around him pulling him in one direction. He faced that way and followed. It led him up the road and around several corners and with each step the tug became stronger so that Toby was forced to run just to ease the pull. It led him around one final corner and there Toby stopped.

The strange force had not led him astray. He had found Maguire.

Chapter Thirty-Four

Just a bit further up the street, Maguire was leaning on the side of a van parked in a driveway. Toby walked toward him just as a man emerged from the house where the van was parked. It was Maguire's father and he was carrying a shovel and a crowbar toward the van.

"Dad, Dad, I got it," Maguire said but was pushed to one side as his father opened the side door of the van and put the tools in.

"Now what was it you wanted?" he asked, finally turning his attention to Maguire.

"I got it."

"Show me."

Maguire reached into his pocket and pulled out Excalibur, still on its chain.

"Good," Maguire's father said as he took it. "Now perhaps I can get that old hag off my back."

He could only mean Morgiana, Toby thought. He didn't know what sort of hold she had over him but it was obviously enough to make him send Maguire out after it.

Toby strode purposely forward.

"That's mine. I want it back."

Maguire's father seemed surprised at first then contemptuous. "Get lost kid."

Toby stopped and planted himself in front of the large man. "Give it back to me please."

Maguire's father snorted. "Out of my way or I'll teach you a lesson"

"Not until you give it back," Toby retorted.

"I'll teach you to give me lip." He swung a backhanded blow which Toby easily dodged under.

"Why you..." He tried to slap the side of Toby's head but again Toby dodged. This only made Maguire's father angrier. He was not used to anyone, particularly a boy, standing up to him.

With a roar he charged at Toby who neatly sidestepped, sending Maguire's father to collide with the side of his van.

"Right," he said to no one in particular as he reached in the van and pulled out the crowbar.

Toby gulped. This was getting serious.

The crowbar waved menacingly and Toby adopted a fighting stance focusing not on the crowbar but the man holding it, tensing and waiting for the first move. It swung and Toby rolled out of the way. It swung again and Toby ducked, feeling the breeze from it ruffle his hair as it passed over his head. That was close. He needed something to defend himself with. He looked longingly at Excalibur still hanging from its chain in Maguire's father's hand and a thought occurred to him.

He jumped back a couple of paces to give himself room and held his hand out. Within moments he felt a comforting pressure in his palm. Maguire's father was distracted by the slight absence of weight in his hand and looked down to see only an empty chain.

By the time he looked back up Toby and Excalibur were ready. Maguire's father only seemed slightly confused by the appearance of the sword and flung the empty chain down in disgust before swinging the crowbar again. Sparks flew where Excalibur struck the crowbar as Toby parried.

Again the crowbar came flying at Toby and again sparks flew where sword and crowbar met. Toby pressed forward feinting to the left causing Maguire's father to defensively raise the crowbar. Toby reversed his motion and swung around, quickly shifting his grip to bring the flat of the blade onto the man's knuckles. With a yelp the man dropped the crowbar and licked his lips nervously as he looked at Toby.

Toby barely had a chance to savour victory before he was grappled from behind. It was Maguire. He'd forgotten all about him during the fight. Toby wriggled, trying to free himself and heard a rip. He quickly looked and noticed his shirt pocket was hanging by a few threads and his notepad was now lying at his feet. This momentary distraction allowed Maguire to secure his grip and now he was trapped as Maguire's arms wrapped around him, holding his arms to his side. Maguire's father, his bravado restored, swaggered forward and grabbed Toby's hand trying to force Excalibur out from his grip.

"I'm going to take this sword, then I am going to give you a sorting to."

Toby, his arms still trapped, forgot about the notepad and focused on this new threat. He remembered one of his first hand to hand combat lessons and he'd asked about rules to make it fair, Caedmon had replied that only a fool put rules on a fight. You fight to survive and to win, not to be fair. With that thought in mind he did the only thing he could think of. He swung his leg up and kicked the man as hard as he could between the legs.

The man crumpled to his knees and Toby heard Maguire gasp in surprise. He used the distraction to fling his head back and was released as the back of his head crunched satisfyingly on Maguire's nose. Maguire staggered back and fell to his knees, cupping his now bloody nose in his hands while his father rolled in agony on the ground.

Toby stared down at them and held Excalibur aloft. "This is Excalibur. It is mine by right. Do not try to take it from me again." He picked up the discarded chain and hung it around his neck then without giving them another glance began to walk home.

◇◇◇◇◇◇

Toby was still charged with adrenaline from his encounter with Maguire and his father and it wasn't until his mother pointed at his ripped pocket that he remembered it happening in the fight. He was still wound up about it and now that was being compounded by needing to spend the whole time until after dinner explaining how his shirt got ripped. Add to that his panic about losing the notebook and he was just about a nervous wreck.

Not wishing to even mention Maguire and his father, he blamed it all on the incident at school. After he'd told them the details they immediately made a call to the school. The fact someone was still there was almost proof enough but after the principal confirmed Toby's story their look of astonishment was also tinged with a bit of guilt.

His mother served dinner as his parents continued to discuss this between themselves occasionally throwing a question at Toby. Finally Toby excused himself on the pretext of wanting a shower and headed for his room. As he passed the lounge he caught the last few minutes of the news on the television and it immediately grabbed his attention.

◇◇◇◇◇◇

On the screen behind the news readers was a large picture of the moon.

"And finally for all you amateur astronomers," the newsreader read. "Don't forget that there is a lunar eclipse tonight. The Earth's shadow will start eating away at the moon at about quarter past nine and should completely cover the moon just after eleven."

The words from the news bulletin ran through his head. That was it.

The Earth's shadow will begin covering the moon. The moon was often called the lesser light so when the prophecy said "When earth consumes the lesser light" it meant the Earth. A lunar eclipse and that meant that whatever was going to happen would happen tonight.

He had to see Merlin.

∞∞∞∞∞

Toby showered and readied himself, apparently, for bed. He went downstairs and pretended to watch television for a while but pretended to fall asleep in his chair. The plan worked and his mother sent him up to bed.

He lay in bed struggling to stay awake in the dark until he heard his door creak open and felt his mother's presence as she came and checked on him. Satisfied she left, quietly closing the door behind her. Toby waited another five minutes to be sure then sprang into action.

He quickly changed and bulked his bed up with whatever he could grab to make it look like he was in it in case she looked in again. He quietly opened the window and climbed out. It was not something he'd done often but like any boy, he'd explored the possibility of sneaking out and thankfully the people who built their house had conveniently placed a downpipe near his window. It offered enough purchase for him to safely climb down.

He ran as fast as he could to the cave where the surprised look on Merlin's face turned to one of alarm as Toby breathlessly said "it's tonight."

Chapter Thirty-Five

"Time is short," said Merlin. "But there's no need to panic. It's not as if any one else can sit there and claim the throne."

The niggle of doubt exploded in Toby's mind. In the courtroom he'd handed Excalibur to Morton. From the sudden look of horror on Merlin's face he'd remembered the same thing.

"Still they don't know where or when to look so..."

Toby groaned. His notepad containing the prophecy, Maguire had probably found it after the fight and would have passed it on. "I think they do," he said and quickly outlined this afternoons events

Merlin was amazingly calm.

"This explains much but for now we must focus on getting there first."

"But..." Toby began thinking that the mountain was an hour's drive away and there was no way they could get there in time.

"Sit on the floor and hold your knees," Merlin snapped. "And pray that this works."

Merlin lit five candles that were evenly spread around the walls of the cave. Each was a different colour and each gave off a pungent yet different smell.

He returned to the centre and stood over Toby placing his hands on either side of Toby's head.

"Think of the place," Merlin instructed as he began muttering under his breath.

The walls blurred and Toby felt as though he was being pulled in several directions at once

There was a moment of panic when he felt weightless

then everything returned to normal.

Merlin stopped muttering, let go of Toby's head and went over to his table where he began mixing something in a cup.

"All things being well, we should be there."

Toby stood up and immediately wished he hadn't. His head spun and his stomach flip flopped several times. He lurched outside where he lent against a tree and was violently sick. He was only vaguely aware of Merlin as he held a cup to his lips and made him drink. The liquid was sweet and soothing and within seconds Toby felt completely normal. He realised for the first time that they were in the picnic area at the base of the hill.

"If you're feeling ready," Merlin said. "We should probably go."

Toby looked up and noticed for the first time the moon had almost vanished.

"We should just make it," Toby said and began the climb toward the peak.

It was a struggle to follow the trail in the dark and Toby stumbled several times.

◇◇◇◇◇◇

As the eclipse became full, the moon turned a dull orange. Toby expected this and could even recall the diagram from the news explaining it. Then something unexpected happened. The moon turned blood red and the hill was bathed in red light.

"Blood of the Pendragon," Merlin observed. "And we are not alone."

In the strange red moonlight Toby could plainly see Morgiana and Morton at the peak. They appeared to be waiting.

It was bright enough now that Toby could easily make out the trail, then the light changed.

It was as though the moon had detached itself from the sky. A glowing orb of red, the source of the light, floated down and headed for the stone seat. This is what they must be waiting for, thought Toby.

He started to run as fast as he could. Even though he had not quite made up his mind about being king he did know one thing. Morton on the throne with Morgiana the power behind it would not be good and he was going to do everything he could to stop that from happening.

As he ran, he kept his eyes on the track so he wouldn't trip on its uneven surface but glanced up every chance he could to judge the descent of the orb. Morgiana finally spotted them.

She frowned and whispered something to Morton before taking a few steps back down the hill toward them. There she cupped her hand and a ball of crackling blue energy appeared. She flung it at Toby but he managed to narrowly dodge it only to see Morgiana with another one ready to throw at him. The path wasn't wide enough for him to keep dodging.

He held his hand out and summoned Excalibur just in time to use it to deflect the ball of energy whizzing his way. He continued up the hill deflecting every single one Morgiana threw at him but each one he deflected slowed him down a bit and Toby realised this was probably her plan. The orb was getting lower and he could only hope he still had enough time. Then he felt one whiz past his ear, only this one was headed up, Merlin must have decided to join the fray.

Morgiana easily dodged it but it meant she wasn't sending one down so Toby could up his pace a bit.

Racing up the final part of the hill, Toby saw the orb descend its final few metres and touch the stone seat. The seat absorbed it like a sponge and began to glow. He was going to be too late. Toby put on an extra burst of speed but he was never going to make it

Morton positioned himself and prepared to sit down, a grin of triumph clearly visible on his face. Toby did the only thing he could think of. He flung Excalibur as hard as he could.

The sword cut a silvery arc in the air as the glowing red light flashed off its blade. Morgiana turned toward him and gasped as she saw Excalibur flying her way. Morton leapt away from the rock just as Excalibur struck point first. A blinding flash of light burst forth forcing everyone to cover their eyes while a cracking noise echoed off the surrounding hills. As the dust settled, they all looked. Arthur's seat was no more. Pieces of it were scattered around the hilltop. Only one large fragment remained and Excalibur stood upright, embedded in it.

The blast had flung both Morton and Morgiana to the ground. Toby arrived at the summit just as they were getting to their feet. Morton was the first to recover. He ran over to the sword and grabbed its hilt as though trying to resurrect a final victory. Vainly, he tried pulling at it. It would not budge. He looked to Morgiana for some encouragement but she shook her head. Her whole posture indicated defeat.

Toby strode past them and, with a huge grin, plucked the sword from the stone.

"Well that would appear to settle that!" Merlin observed.

Chapter Thirty-Six

It was six weeks later and Toby was once again beside the lake where it had all begun, only this time Merlin was standing beside him.

Toby had woken the morning after the mountain top battle, not even remembering how he'd gotten home. He presumed Merlin had made the cave travel to behind his wardrobe again and as that would have made him sick again, he was rather glad he couldn't remember.

He did remember the devastated look on the face of Morgiana, though Morton, when he thought Morgiana wasn't looking, looked relieved and actually gave Toby an apologetic grin before they trudged off.

Merlin had spent quite a while poking and prodding the remains of the stone seat. He kept staring off into space and muttering as though reading something invisible before shaking his head in annoyance and poking and prodding a bit more. But beyond that, Toby couldn't recall anything.

◇◇◇◇◇◇

He didn't even make it to his first class the following morning. Someone must have been keeping a lookout for him because as soon as he was in the gates he was directed to the principal's office and ushered in without waiting.

He was surprised to see Brook already seated in the office and anger boiled inside about the betrayal he felt. The only bit of satisfaction was that she was here and probably in trouble. Brook seemed pleased to see him but one look at his face and she stopped smiling and faced the desk.

Mr Hautler indicated for him to sit and as he did so he couldn't help but notice a thick file on the desk with his name prominently on the cover.

"You seem to have a habit of causing trouble Mr Cooper," the principal said indicating the file.

"Now first I would like to discuss last night. Miss Sonnet has given me an account and Brook here has..."

Toby scowled and gave Brook another dirty look.

"I find your attitude to Brook surprising," Mr Hautler said, reacting to Toby's look. "Because if this young lady hadn't bashed on my office window last night, then I wouldn't have witnessed Mr Lloyd's behaviour myself and I daresay would have been just adding another entry into your considerable file."

So that's where she'd run off too. Toby was mortified. She hadn't betrayed him she'd been helping.

"Sorry I..." He looked beseechingly at Brook and after a moments hesitation she gave him a forgiving smile.

"I'm glad to see that's sorted," Mr Hautler continued dryly. "So I will move on.

"It appears your troublesome nature only reared its ugly head at the school camp, at least that is when Mr Lloyd started making copious notes about you,"

Mr Hautler flipped idly through the file making Toby nervous.

"So I guess that would be a good place to start."

Toby hesitated. While he was glad Mr Lloyd had been caught out, he was still unsure about confessing everything from the camp as he hadn't been completely blameless. In the end he decided to tell everything (everything related to the camp at least) including the great food robbery.

Brook looked horrified as he told details of their scheme although Mr Hautler's only reaction was to raise one eyebrow and comment that they had at least stolen healthy food.

Toby eventually ran out of things to say and went quiet, sitting nervously as Mr Hautler looked pensively at him across his bridged fingers.

"Thank you for your honesty Toby," he said as he finally broke the silence. "There will be repercussions from your actions but I assure you, they will not be serious." Brook breathed a huge sigh of relief.

"For now," he continued, "I would like you both to go to class and focus on your schoolwork."

◇◇◇◇◇◇◇

Brook caught up to Toby in the corridor.

"Wait," she said as she caught him by the arm. "About what you said in there."

Toby was all set for an angry outburst for telling about Brook's part in the food theft but instead. "You didn't tell him everything did you? You didn't say anything about the lake."

"What!" said Toby, completely caught of guard.

"The lake, don't tell me there was nothing. I followed you one morning."

Toby remembered. The morning he'd nearly woken Peter, he thought he'd been followed but had put it down to nerves.

"You went round a corner and vanished. What was going on? I know it wasn't anything secret to do with your friends because they're not that good at keeping secrets. So what was it?"

Toby tried to think of something to say that would explain everything but couldn't so he tried a bluff.

"You wouldn't believe me if I told you."

"Try me!" was the immediate response. So he did.

"You're right, I don't," she said as he finished. "I have never heard such a load of rubbish. Why didn't you say 'mind your own business' instead of..." and then she stopped.

Toby had raised his hand and was now holding Excalibur in front of her.

"Oh!" she said and without thinking, reached out

227

her hand toward it before withdrawing. "It doesn't want me to touch it," she said in amazement as she dropped her hand away.

"Please don't tell," Toby implored as they made their way to class and Brook could only nod her assent.

◇◇◇◇◇◇

In the weeks that followed, several things happened

Their punishment for stealing was announced. They were not permitted to attend the inter school football grand final. Most thought this seemed a harsh but fair punishment. Toby thought of it as a reward as he had to spend the time in the school library with only Brook for company. In fact he seemed to be spending a lot of time with Brook which was the source of much teasing from Peter.

The team lost the grand final but the trophy cabinet did not stay empty as Peter won the tennis competition. He was paraded in front of a school assembly as a champion, which allowed Toby to get in a bit of return teasing.

The final thing was the announcement of another school camp to make up for the last one but this time making sure everyone had a good time and so Toby was back at the lake with Merlin.

"It's time Toby," Merlin said. "Excalibur has served its purpose and now must be returned."

Toby nodded. Merlin had explained that Excalibur was only on loan until such time as it was no longer needed and with the prophecy passing in such an unusual fashion, that time was now. It would be returned to the lake just as it had been in the past.

Toby raised his hand and took a long last look at Excalibur as it appeared there. He drew his arm back preparing to throw, and then frowned.

"Somehow I don't think I'm finished yet," he said and with that he released Excalibur and it vanished, returning to its now normal position around his neck.

Merlin cast a critical eye over the lake then gave Toby a sideways look.

"Prophecies be damned," he finally said. "But I think you may be right." He patted Toby on the shoulder before walking off to leave Toby staring out over the calm waters of the lake.

The future lay ahead and now, not even Merlin knew how it would unfold.

The End

www.ingramcontent.com/pod-product-compliance
Lightning Source LLC
Chambersburg PA
CBHW020833260626
47169CB00003B/964